D0652239

URBAN GUERRILLAS

Pressed up against the corridor wall, John Rourke could almost pinpoint the origin of Rausch's voice. Something was wrong, Rausch was acting carelessly.

Just before Rourke's fingertips touched the metal on the door handle, he drew his hand back and took the Zippo from his pocket. Rourke shielded the lighter with his body, then crouched beside the doorway. Two thin wires ran from the doorknob's base. Rourke's eyes followed the wires down to the base of the door, then along the molding on the wall; they ended at the wall outlet.

John Rourke unsheathed his LS-X knife and went to work on the wires. He smiled. He was ahead of the game . . . for now!

THE SURVIVALIST SERIES
by Jerry Ahern

#1: TOTAL WAR	(2445, $2.95)
#2: THE NIGHTMARE BEGINS	(2476, $2.95)
#3: THE QUEST	(2670, $2.95)
#4: THE DOOMSAYER	(0893, $2.50)
#5: THE WEB	(2672, $2.95)
#6: THE SAVAGE HORDE	(2937, $2.95)
#7: THE PROPHET	(1339, $2.50)
#8: THE END IS COMING	(2590, $2.95)
#9: EARTH FIRE	(2938, $2.95)
#10: THE AWAKENING	(1478, $2.50)
#11: THE REPRISAL	(2393, $2.95)
#12: THE REBELLION	(2777, $2.95)
#13: PURSUIT	(2477, $2.95)
#14: THE TERROR	(2775, $2.95)
#15: OVERLORD	(2070, $2.50)

Available wherever paperbacks are sold, or order direct from the Publisher. Send cover price plus 50¢ per copy for mailing and handling to Zebra Books, Dept. 2990, 475 Park Avenue South, New York, N.Y. 10016. Residents of New York, New Jersey and Pennsylvania must include sales tax. DO NOT SEND CASH.

#20

THE SURVIVALIST

FIRESTORM

BY JERRY AHERN

ZEBRA BOOKS
KENSINGTON PUBLISHING CORP.

This is a work of fiction. All the characters and events portrayed in this book are fictional, and any resemblance to real people or incidents is purely coincidental.

ZEBRA BOOKS

are published by

Kensington Publishing Corp.
475 Park Avenue South
New York, NY 10016

Copyright © 1990 by Jerry Ahern

All rights reserved. No part of this book may be reproduced in any form or by any means without the prior written consent of the Publisher, excepting brief quotes used in reviews.

First printing: May, 1990

Printed in the United States of America

For our friend, Billy Frank Agee, the sort of true man John Rourke would be proud to call friend. All the best . . .

Chapter One

The grazing gunshot wound across John Rourke's shoulder blades stung him more than hurt him, numbness setting in at the center of his back, but merely the body's defense mechanisms against pain, his physician's training made him realize. And he was cold, a combination of weather conditions and, he thought, possibly shock. There was no time after the battle to repel the Soviet attack against Eden Base for him to treat the wound, six or seven of the Elite Corpsmen who had escaped the battlefield having fled into miles of the long, narrow band of dense evergreen woods which struck northward toward the mountains like a scar, a frozen creek bed bisecting it along its length. But if it were shock setting in, he did what he could to minimize it, the hood of his parka up and secured, his coat closed all the way, gloves on. And he moved slowly, trying not to tax his strength, saving his body's resources for what might happen when he found the KGB Elite Corpsmen.

Rourke's fists were tight on his M-16, his other guns reloaded, holstered. His eyes followed the fast-filling-in footprints in the snow. Six or seven sets of male footprints, so jumbled he could not discern the exact number. But had it been only these, he would have let the men go. German aircraft aplenty were available for an aerial search that would eventually discover them, despite the poor visibility from the falling snow and the coming of night.

Eventually was the key word, however. There was a complication which imparted added urgency to the chase: An extra set of footprints. A woman's. One of the women who had been among the Eden Base defenders and who had left the defensive position by the breach in the wall to join him in the counter-attack was not accounted for. No body lying on the battlefield or listed among the many wounded at the bomb-damaged field hospital.

Her name, Rourke learned, was Maritza Zeiss, one of the West

German members of the international astronaut corps which comprised Eden Base personnel. The tread pattern of the woman's bootprints he followed matched that of the boots worn by Eden personnel, distinctly different than the tread pattern of the Soviet footgear.

There was a German helicopter gunship landing near the re-entrant, the line of woods made into the snowpacked plain which led toward Eden Base and the road which had served as the Eden Project landing field. The ruined and, at least temporarily, abandoned German base was visible in the distance.

John Rourke stopped there, the Mid-Wake submarine commander Captain Jason Darkwood shivering beside him. "I'm used to more controlled climatic conditions, Doctor. Forgive the noise of my chattering teeth."

"Merely a natural body defense, the body trying to generate heat through motion. My teeth are chattering a little bit, too," Rourke observed, watching the helicopter more intently now as his friend, Paul Rubenstein, exited it, running toward them out of the swirl of artificial blizzard created by the downdraft of the whirring rotor blades.

"You should be getting that wound treated, John!" Paul Rubenstein shouted as he jogged toward them jockeying his German MP-40 submachinegun and his M-16 back on their slings so he could close his coat.

"News travels fast," Rourke told his friend.

The younger man smiled, a second later the smile vanishing behind the black knit toque Paul Rubenstein pulled over his head and face. "Well, I spoke with Elaine Halversen on the radio. She told me what you guys were up to out here. Sam Aldridge sent Lieutenant St. James's platoon by chopper a few miles farther north. Michael's with them. Aldridge figured to cut the Elite Corpsmen off."

"Good," John Rourke nodded. "We'll have to keep in radio contact so we don't wind up shooting each other. It'll be dark soon," Rourke observed, adding, "Or, I should say 'darker'."

The weather had been deteriorating, if that were possible, throughout the day, conditions going from annoying to intolerable to dangerous. With the conventional avionics of five centuries ago, no helicopter would have dared fly. "Let's treat your wound aboard the gunship, all right? We'll make better time because of it in the long run," Paul declared.

John Rourke just looked at his friend. "Suddenly you're the doctor?"

Paul shrugged. "You know it makes sense."

Rourke nodded. "We do it fast," then started toward the black German gunship . . .

Akiro Kurinami, looking as if he were about to pass out from exhaustion, knelt beside her where she sat with her back to the wall.

Fewer than a dozen feet from her was the body of the man she'd shot, as he was about to shoot Akiro Kurinami in the back.

Colonel Mann and Commander Dodd, on opposite sides of the body, stood over it.

She could hear them talking, her eyes moving to the Trapper Scorpion .45 which was still in her hand, the slide locked back, open over the empty magazine. She'd shot the man until the gun was fired out.

Since the Night of the War, she'd killed many people in defense of herself or defense of others. But there was something very different, scarily unnerving about this. The man she'd killed had clearly been about to cold-bloodedly murder Akiro.

Why?

Sarah Rourke tuned her thoughts, with some difficulty, toward the conversation continuing between Colonel Mann and Commander Dodd.

" . . . that she was mistaken. After all, Mrs. Rourke is under considerable strain. She's pregnant, and—"

"Commander, if Frau Rourke indicated that she shot this man, Damien Rausch, an escaped Nazi criminal, because he was attempting to murder Lieutenant Kurinami, then that is exactly the way that it happened."

"You keep saying he's a Nazi of some kind," Dodd said, shaking his head, "but how can you be sure? I mean, did you memorize the face of every one of the men in the Nazi party after it was deposed?"

Wolfgang Mann sighed audibly. "There were two men at the hierarchy of the leader's party elite. They were brothers. This man,

Damien Rausch, and Freidrich Rausch, were the very elite of that elite. You have, no doubt, heard of the SS?"

"That was five hundred years ago, Colonel."

"But the pattern of organization within the Nazi party which dominated my nation until Herr Doctor Rourke assisted us in at last attaining freedom," Wolfgang said, an edge in his voice that made Sarah think his patience was near its end, "was identical to that of the Nazi era in the 1930s and 1940s in Old Germany. The SS were the leader's political police and eternal stalwarts." And then he looked from Commander Dodd toward Sarah, Sarah's eyes meeting his. "The brothers Rausch were the most vile and despicable of the leader's minions. They would never surrender their beliefs in the ultimate triumph of National Socialism. And, if Freidrich Rausch still lives, he will never surrender the desire to kill Frau Rourke for killing his brother." It was cold there by the wall, the snow hard driven on the wind.

Sarah Rourke shivered . . .

Paul was right, of course. The alternating stinging and numbness was gone, John Rourke's wound cleaned and treated. And taking a fresh parka from the gunship helped, one without the added ventilation made by the rifle bullet, helped against the cold nearly as much as the knowledge that the wound was even less serious than John Rourke had suspected.

With Paul Rubenstein and Jason Darkwood flanking him, all three of them with their weapons at the ready, they moved through the woods now.

As Rourke had feared, the footprints were harder to follow because they were harder to discern, the blowing snow filling them almost too rapidly. But here and there, where one of the tall pines would break the wind, there was sign.

They kept going, the sparsely scattered footprints following the line of the frozen creek. It was rocky here, as if the creek bed were a gouge and the material moved aside for its creation had been strewn about haphazardly to either side of it.

Rourke's strength was returning to him as he got his second wind, beyond tired now.

There had been no tracks visible for nearly a quarter mile and

John Rourke was just about to concede that the fleeing KGB Elite Corpsmen and their hostage had gone deeper into the woods, leaving the course of the creek bed. But then, as his flashlight, one of the very powerful German ones, shifted right, Rourke saw something in the high, smooth rocks near the center of the creek bed.

It was clearly a footprint.

"Paul, give me a hand down there," Rourke said, shivering as an errant gust of wind breached the left side of his parka hood when he turned.

"You see something?"

"I think it's a track, there in the cleft in the rocks. Empty your M-16, Paul."

As John Rourke checked his M-16's condition of readiness—he wanted it on safe for the climb downward—he moved toward the embankment. Jason Darkwood spoke into his radio set. "This is Captain Darkwood calling scouting party. Come in. Over."

Rourke didn't wait to have the transmission relayed to him, starting down over the ice-coated rocks of the creek bank, Paul Rubenstein wedged above him, holding an emptied M-16 by the buttstock as Rourke edged downward, moving his hands along the front handguard then down along the barrel toward the flash deflector.

The footing was dangerously uncertain and Rourke moved slowly, cautiously. To break or twist an ankle now would benefit no one. He could faintly hear Darkwood. "We're proceeding as planned, Lieutenant. What's your status? Over."

There was nothing for it but to drop the remaining three feet to the level of the creek unless he wanted to climb back up and start down again with a rope. Rourke elected to jump, letting go of Paul's rifle, coming down in a crouch on the ice-coated dirt and gravel, slipping, catching himself on both hands, his rifle's buttstock banging against a rock.

Cautiously, Rourke moved to a standing position, his eyes, now with the aid of the flashlight again, shifting back and forth over the stream bed, trying to place the cleft of rock he had seen from above from this different perspective. He had it, walking very slowly out onto the frozen ripples of the creek surface. His M-16, still on safe, was in his left hand, Rourke tapping gently against the surface of the ice with its muzzle, like a blind man might have used a cane five centuries ago.

11

Today, there were still persons who were blind, but none who could not see, with the possible exception of the Wild Tribes of Europe. Both the technologies of New Germany and of Mid-Wake had arrived at the same methodology, utilizing video sensing lenses in what looked largely like ordinary sunglasses, the microcircuitry in the frames processing the signals and translating them to electro-magnetic impulses readable within the vision centers of the optic thalmus. He'd been fortunate to read three papers on the subject, two in English and one, translated for him from the technical German which was so difficult that it was impossible to enjoy without the translation.

Rourke ceased walking and musing simultaneously as his eyes focused on the imprint revealed in the snow-filled niche in the rocks under the yellow-white beam of his flashlight. It was a deep handprint, the length of the digits and the overall span of the hand, taking into account that it would have been gloved, clearly belonging to a woman.

Rourke raised his voice to a loud whisper, but of sufficient volume that Paul, who was watching him, would be able to hear. "They crossed the stream. Come on."

Chapter Two

The snow fell more lightly here in the tall pines, the boughs above him weighted almost to the breaking point. Occasionally, a bough would partially collapse under the weight and snow by what seemed the bucketful would fall, covering his parka hood, his shoulders, his equipment.

He circumscribed a small clearing clockwise, Paul Rubenstein doing the same, but counterclockwise.

Rourke rolled back the storm sleeve of his parka, his right hand cupping around the lens of the flashlight, nearly covering it as he turned his back toward the far side of the clearing. The Rolex on his wrist confirmed the count he had kept in his head. Five minutes had passed. A radio communication from Lieutenant St. James had, only moments before that, confirmed what Rourke's tracking, easier here in the deeper woods on the far side of the stream, had intimated. The Elite Corpsmen were tiring, slowing. From a vantage point among high rocks nearly a mile away, using sophisticated light-gathering binoculars, Lieutenant St. James's Marines had spotted the group. Eight persons in all, translating to seven Elite Corpsmen and their female hostage. They had stopped to rest.

As Rourke switched the beam off his flashlight and turned around, Jason Darkwood promptly entered the very edge of the clearing, half its width behind Rourke's own position now.

The instructions to Lieutenant St. James had been simple. Advance in a long skirmish line, making a lot of noise, forcing the quarry to either move back the way they had come or take a defensive position.

Either way, their backs would be turned in the direction from which Rourke, Paul Rubenstein and Darkwood were coming. Darkwood's crossing the clearing more or less openly was insur-

13

ance. Unless the Elite Corpsmen were imbeciles, they'd be watching their backs and spot Darkwood.

John Rourke began moving again, slowly, silently, drawing the Life Support System X from its sheath at his side, his gloved hand fisting it in a rapier hold as he moved through the snow . . .

Jason Darkwood's palms sweated inside his heavy gloves. He'd done the thing every midshipman learned not to do: volunteer. He was the best man for the job because he was the least experienced in surface warfare, a novice compared to veterans like Doctor Rourke and Mr. Rubenstein.

Rubenstein was an interesting guy, Darkwood thought. Talk about truth to the old expression of not judging a book by its cover. Paul Rubenstein wasn't short, but he wasn't exactly tall, either. His hair was thinning badly. He didn't seem overtly muscular. And suddenly, as he walked (hopefully obviously, since if he were running the risk of getting shot it should be for a good reason) he found himself thinking about Rubenstein's very pretty wife, Annie. Doctor Rourke's daughter, she had the Rourke way about her, commanding, yet she was marvelously feminine and very refreshing. Mr. Rubenstein was a lucky man.

Darkwood stopped beside a tall tree with snow on its bark. Snow fascinated him, the very look of it, its taste on the tongue.

He realized that this, the reality of life, was something everyone at Mid-Wake missed, most without ever realizing it. In five centuries of living beneath the sea in a domed complex, traveling within the city or, for persons like himself who were part of Mid-Wake's defense forces, traveling by submarine, but always within a controlled environment, generations had been spent this way. But with Mid-Wake's unavoidable involvement now in the surface war against the Russians of the Underground City in the Ural Mountains, it was the end of an era.

In one respect, that was good. The stringent, voluntary population control (with the help of five centuries of war casualties) which had kept Mid-Wake numbers manageable for five centuries would someday, perhaps soon, be unnecessary. There was an entire world to populate, to know, to experience.

And, if he lived that long, he wanted very much to be part of that. Unexplored seas. And, what shores did they kiss?

Good thoughts.

He resumed walking, the M-16 he'd grabbed up from the hands of a dead Eden Base defender still unfamiliar to his hands.

Darkwood compromised, shifting the assault rifle into his left hand, drawing the Mid-Wake issue pistol. He knew what a 9mm Lancer Caseless would do to an enemy from firsthand experience, the M-16 only through observation.

The 2418 A2 had a solid feel to it, largely psychological he knew, but much of warfare, much of survival was psychological.

Somewhere in the woods on either side of the clearing which he skirted, Doctor Rourke and Mr. Rubenstein were closing on the enemy.

If he couldn't tell exactly where they were, did that mean the enemy couldn't either?

The enemy. For five centuries, the people of Mid-Wake had fought the forces of the Soviet underwater complex which shared, ironically, the same undersea volcanic vent as a source of geothermal energy.

There were some in Mid-Wake, Darkwood had heard, who blamed Doctor Rourke for involving Mid-Wake in the war on the land, with these new Soviet enemies. But these were the uninformed who let one too many drinks do the talking for them, or were mindless to begin with. Once the Soviet Navy had nuclear missile capabilities, as had been proven conclusively, a broadening of the five centuries long war was inevitable. There was no danger of direct nuclear attack on Mid-Wake, the serendipity of that shared volcanic vent geothermal power source the mitigating factor there. But Soviet Island Class submarines armed with nuclear missiles could have destroyed the Mid-Wake fleet, leaving Mid-Wake powerless to resist Soviet invasion by any other means than flooding.

The flooding of Mid-Wake was a popular topic among some of the very old. Once, when the Soviet Marine Spetznas had attacked Mid-Wake in force, better than seventy years ago, it was said that when all had seemed lost, when it seemed the people of Mid-Wake were close to extinction, the government had been on the verge of flooding the city, stopping the Soviets, killing everyone, collapsing the domes under the pressure of the sea around them.

It would have come to that because, with the Soviet collective system and selective genetic breeding it was possible for the Soviets to produce a disproportionate number of male offspring, the vast majority of the Soviet forces, both Naval and Marine Spetznas, male. Not only was the Soviet population greater, but its percentage of fighting men out of all proportion to actual population numbers.

Inevitable.

Darkwood reached the midway point in the clearing.

If someone was going to start shooting at him, it would be soon, now. His gloved fist tightened on the butt of the 2418 A2. "God," he muttered under his breath. He wished he was back aboard his submarine . . .

John Rourke stood stock still. Movement at about eleven o'clock on the far side of the clearing. Paul might have seen it, but that was doubtful from Paul's vantage point on the opposite side coming up from the six o'clock position counterclockwise.

He couldn't wait for a gunshot, because Darkwood was risking his neck enough and one shot or a full-automatic burst could be the end of the man. And Darkwood was a good man, despite the sometimes flippant demeanor.

John Rourke dropped into a crouch, moving forward quickly now, the LS-X still in the rapier hold.

Movement again, perhaps fifty yards off, snow dislodging and falling to the ground.

John Rourke moved laterally, deeper into the trees, as he increased the distance between himself and whoever had moved ahead of him, rising to his full height, quickening his pace. He reached the apex of the triangle of his movement pattern, working his way between the trees and through the sporadic high drifts, snow crunching under his boots but the noise unavoidable without losing more valuable time.

He kept going, seeing movement again, ahead and to the left of him, from the same spot where he had first seen it. But from this angle, he could see its origin more clearly. A man, roughly his own height, in the black battle uniform of the KGB Elite Corps, an assault rifle in his hands, halfway to his shoulder as though he were just ready to snap off a burst.

John Rourke promised himself something. He started to move, a long-strided run across the snow, the Crain knife in his right fist, the man with the assault rifle starting to turn around, John Rourke hurtling himself toward him, the knife beside Rourke's right hip, then arcing forward into the Elite Corpsman's abdomen, primary edge up. As Rourke's left hand closed over the man's mouth, Rourke's body blocking the rifle from being raised, Rourke's right hand tensed, his forearm pulsing with exertion as he tore the knife upward from navel to sternum, a sound almost like a sigh, muffled beneath Rourke's gloved hand, the Elite Corpsman's body going rigid, then suddenly limp.

John Rourke was up, to his feet, wiping the blade of his knife clean of blood against the snow-splotched bark of a tree.

He heard movement seventy-five or a hundred yards deeper into the woods, saw snow crashing down from a low hanging bough on the far side of the clearing, at approximately two o'clock.

Paul.

John Rourke broke left, into a long-strided run.

More movement, a rasped caution in Russian, the howl of the wind, like the moaning of a ghost from a horrific nightmare, a splotch of black uniform against a drift of white snow.

There was a woman's scream.

Rourke was even with them now and he turned, running toward them from their right flank, shouting, "Paul! Darkwood! Over here!"

His knife was sheathed, his fists closing on the butts of the two Scoremasters.

"John!" It was Paul's voice. "The rest of you, close in from that side. You and you and you, follow me!"

And Darkwood's voice, getting in on the act. "Take the left flank, you and you, and you two. Follow me, the rest of you!"

There was movement, running, a burst of automatic weapons fire lighting the darkness. Rourke prayed it wasn't the woman being put to death.

There was an aggregate of rocks, open to the far and near sides, affording protection from the direction of the clearing and the direction from which Lieutenant Lillie St. James's platoon of Marines would be coming.

But no protection from him.

John Rourke saw one of them turn, an assault rifle starting to open up.

Rourke dodged right and back as the Scoremaster in his right hand raised to shoulder height, his right first finger making the squeeze.

Snow churned up before him as the Scoremaster rocked gently in his right fist.

He averted his eyes as the snow sprayed toward him. More assault rifle fire.

Rourke caught a glimpse of a body going down as Rourke's left hand raised to shoulder height, a single shot to the Elite Corpsman nearest the female captive. The Elite Corpsman's left hand flashed to his neck as his body spun back.

Assault rifle fire tore into the tree trunks beside Rourke. Rourke fired both pistols from shoulder height, silencing the rifleman. Rourke dove left, hitting the snow, rolling, the snow beside him plowed up under a fresh burst of assault rifle fire.

He heard Paul shout, "Stay down, John!"

The rattle of Paul Rubenstein's submachine gun, neat three-round bursts, textbook perfect. As Rourke came up to his knees beside a y-shaped pine trunk, he saw one of the remaining three men going down, then a second man down.

The last man swung his rifle toward the woman. Rourke's pistols went up, firing simultaneously, but simultaneously as well, there was gunfire from Rourke's right and from Paul's direction also, the Elite Corpsman's body wheeling back and forth, twisting around, falling.

Rourke looked to his right. Darkwood, pistol in hand, stood there.

"It's Doctor Rourke, Miss Zeiss. Are you all right?"

Rourke started moving forward, Darkwood beside him, Paul circling to the far side so that if anyone were still alive and dangerous they'd have him in a crossfire.

She stumbled out of the rocks, the gleam of blood on her right cheek, possibly hers or perhaps from the rupturing of a gunshot wound near her.

As she fell to her knees, John Rourke nodded to Darkwood, Darkwood dropping to his knees beside her, taking her into his arms.

As John Rourke's eyes scanned the bodies, he heard the crunching of snow under Paul's boots and he heard Jason Darkwood's voice. "I've never seen anyone like you, Doctor."

Rourke didn't say anything, more important things on his mind.

Chapter Three

Natalia Anastasia Tiemerovna heard Annie's voice. She opened her eyes, the brightness making her close them again.

"How you feeling?"

Natalia turned her head away, a flood of memories now, confusing, no clear boundary between what had happened and what had not. Knights in armor, helicopter pursuits, Michael about to be killed, John's knife in her hands and Vladmir's head.

She felt silly as she said it, and her voice sounded oddly dry, disused, unfamiliar to her. "Where am I?"

As she turned her head back and opened her eyes, more slowly this time, Annie almost whispered, "You've been very sick, Natalia. But you're better now. You're in the hospital, at Mid-Wake. A lot of things happened, but everybody's fine, my mom and dad, Paul, Michael, Otto. Everybody. And, now that you're better, well, things will be just great. There's an alliance and we're going to turn things around. I just know it."

Natalia ran her hands back through her hair. Her hair felt just washed, just arranged.

"You have such pretty hair," Annie smiled. "I hope I fixed it right."

"I remember something—you were—"

"It was the only way to make you better, to find out what was wrong. I figured, well, that you would have done anything to help me. So, ahh—"

Annie looked down at her hands which were folded in her lap. Natalia watched her for a moment. Annie wore a print skirt, subdued purple flowers against a background that was so gray it was almost black, a black blouse with long wide sleeves and open at the throat, her hair drawn back from her face. She remembered how John used to call Annie's hair "honey blonde." It was darker now, but so very beautiful.

"Annie. You are my best friend."

Annie moved to the edge of the bed, folding Natalia into her arms, touching her lips to Natalia's forehead. Natalia rested her head against Annie's shoulder.

Chapter Four

John Rourke and his wife stood beside the table, Sarah Rourke's face a little pale, Darkwood thought, compared to the rest of the surface people around. On reflection, it had to have been a terrible experience for her, killing that man a split second before the man would have murdered the Japanese naval lieutenant. Darkwood stripped off his gloves and opened his coat, Sarah Rourke saying to Maritza Zeiss, "I'm so happy it's nothing serious. When they radioed back that they'd found you and you were all right, everyone was so happy."

"Your husband was so brave, Frau—"

John Rourke cut that short. "I just thought I'd check in. Leaving you in good hands," and he nodded toward Darkwood, shot Maritza Zeiss a smile and ushered his wife toward a still open panel on the far wall. They disappeared.

It was a little cold in the tent, despite the heater units working to capacity and the plastic-like material patched over at least most of the holes which were ripped in the tent walls by shrapnel and debris during the battle for Eden. She was stripped to rather male-looking underwear—something like an athletic shirt and panties more the size of shorts—and there was a blanket wrapped around her shoulders. But Jason Darkwood couldn't help thinking that she was really beautiful. He realized he was staring at her, turned away, found a table to perch on the edge of and found himself staring at her again.

Maritza Zeiss cleaned up very nicely.

She'd been badly shaken by her ordeal, but physically unharmed, the German doctor they'd spoken with a moment earlier had told them, unharmed except for a few bruises and the beginnings of frostbite on the tips of the toes of her right foot.

She sat on the edge of an examining table, talking almost unceasingly as a nurse did something to the little toe. Maritza Zeiss' voice was tinged with nervous exhaustion.

"So, you command a submarine? Wow."

"You're German, I know, but you sound very American. Did Germans from five hundred years ago all speak English so well?"

She laughed, winced a little as the nurse daubed something on the toe, said, "I went to college in the United States. Then came back here for my doctorate."

Darkwood realized he was staring at her, smiling at her. She was very pretty, reddish blonde hair, the hint of freckles on her shoulders where the blanket fell away, a long and slender neck and a nice figure. Inside his head, he could hear Maggie Barrow saying, "Right, Jason! You want to get our relationship going again? I bet!" He shrugged his shoulders, to turn off his conscience perhaps. "What did you earn your PhD in?"

"Agriculture."

He started to laugh.

"Why are you laughing?" Maritza Zeiss smiled, pouting her lip a little.

"Well, ahh," and Darkwood smiled. "You're the first five hundred year old farmer I've ever met. I didn't realize farmers were so pretty."

She started to say something and then her jaw literally dropped as there was a crashing sound.

Darkwood started to his feet, toward her, then saw her eyes. She was staring at something behind him and he turned around. One of the volunteers had dropped a tray of instruments and, as the woman bent over, her hand or something must have caught on the sheet covering the gurney behind her. There was a dead body visible, the face blue-veined and gray. Darkwood had seen the body before, when he and John Rourke and Paul Rubenstein had returned to Eden Base, the body just lying on the ground then, like so many others. But the commander of the forces from New Germany, Colonel Wolfgang Mann, and the Eden Project commander, Christopher Dodd, had been standing near it, arguing over something. Sarah Rourke had just been sitting on the ground beside the wall, staring at it, an empty pistol on her lap. It was the body of the Nazi, Damien Rausch, the man that Sarah Rourke had shot to death there at the wall. Maybe the body was about to be autopsied or something.

Darkwood assumed Maritza Zeiss was shocked at the sight of still another casualty, regardless of who it was.

But as he turned around and started to say something comforting, Maritza Zeiss said, "That is the man I saw with Commander Dodd. Poor man. Commander Dodd said he was an agent working for Colonel Mann. He probably died very bravely."

Jason Darkwood looked at her as he said very softly, "His was a unique death, I understand. Yes."

He looked back at the lividinous countenance as the man who'd dropped the instruments, having them under control now, threw the black plastic sheet back over the dead man's face. "Very unique," Darkwood whispered.

Chapter Five

John Rourke stood just inside the hermetic flap of the tent, snow already dripping off the shoulders of his parka. He'd been offered a seat, refused, then told Dodd why he'd come. From an inside pocket, he took one of his cigars, rolling it in his fingertips, watching Commander Christopher Dodd in the light from the overhead lamp.

"I'd like to confront her. That's what I'd like to do!" Dodd almost shouted, thudding his open palm down on the folding camp table. He was an unconvincing actor. "This Zeiss woman must have had more of a shock with being taken hostage like that than anyone suspected. If she can say what she said to your precious Captain Darkwood to my face, I'll step down as Eden Base commander, Doctor Rourke. And I know that'd make certain elements here—like Kurinami and Halversen and yourself and your family—exceedingly happy."

"Well, you're right there," John Rourke said, looking at him. The wound across Rourke's shoulder blades didn't pain him at all, but it itched. The German spray which acted at once as a healing agent and disinfectant worked, sometimes too well. "If she is incorrect, I'll owe you an apology for even mentioning this."

Dodd's eyes narrowed and he stood up from behind the table. "If she's correct, Doctor, I'd be a traitor, wouldn't I? So, if I had anything to hide, why the hell would I want to confront her in the first place? Answer me that, if you can! Think about it, man! Just because some of my decisions around here are unpopular, everybody wants to see me get tossed in the trash pile. And I'm sick of it. I'll confront her, all right! She's either lying or crazy. That—what was his name?"

John Rourke lit the cigar. He looked across the blue yellow flame from his old battered Zippo and almost whispered, "Damien

Rausch."

"Rausch. Yes. That man may have been drifting in and out of camp here. For all I know, he could have been wearing a German uniform. Most of those—"

"They all look alike?" John Rourke supplied.

"That's not what I meant, damnit."

"She's in her tent, Doctor Zeiss that is. Why don't we walk over there and see her. Under the circumstances, considering her ordeal, it'd be the polite thing."

Dodd looked at the watch on his wrist, hesitated, then nodded. "All right. I'll go with you. Let me get my coat."

John Rourke only nodded . . .

Paul looked like a snowman. He hadn't wanted to come inside Dodd's tent and had stood outside under the canopy shelter. But the wind blew quite strongly and the snow fell heavily, the result Paul's parka was covered. He patted his sleeves to get rid of some of the snow as they walked, the three of them abreast, Paul to Rourke's right, Dodd to Rourke's left. Brushing away the snow was a useless gesture, Rourke thought, because already his own parka was all but covered with it, as was Dodd's, and Paul's was re-covering.

They walked across the camp in silence, Rourke puffing on his cigar, Paul still brushing away snow.

Maritza Zeiss' tent, which she shared with five other women, was on the far side of the base, near the north perimeter. Although much had been destroyed there, the tent was spared.

German troops moved about the area near the prefabricated perimeter wall, repairing it, Eden Base personnel assisting them. There was no way to tell when the Russians might strike again, although logic, substantiated by German high altitude electronic intelligence, dictated it wouldn't be soon. There weren't enough gunships in any one place that massing for an attack seemed in progress.

Rourke saw the tent ahead.

Dodd asked, "Is that it? I hope so; I'm freezing."

Rourke looked at him, saying nothing, exhaling smoke, the smoke lost in the steam of his breath.

They reached the tent, the crunching of snow under their boots stopping. Rourke's eyes swept over the ground. He thought he detected footprints seeming to come from inside the tent, but the wind drove the snow so strongly that he couldn't be sure.

Paul looked at him. Rourke nodded. Paul took his gloved right hand from the muff pocket and rapped on the tent pole beside the hermetically sealed door. "Doctor Zeiss? It's us, John Rourke and Paul Rubenstein. We have Dodd with us."

Rourke looked at the hermetically sealed flap, then dropped to one knee before it, tugging off his right outer glove, drawing his first finger through the nearly filled depression in the snow, the depression which could have been a bootprint. "Try again, Paul."

"Doctor Zeiss? Captain Darkwood?"

"Evidently she's out," Dodd said, his voice holding a hint of sarcasm.

Rourke looked up, then stood, dusting snow from his inner glove. "Probably ducked out for a pizza." John Rourke started opening the tent flap, raising his voice, saying, "We're coming inside," then to Paul, his voice lowering, "Watch out."

As Rourke pulled open the flap with his left hand, his right hand found the butt of one of the Scoremasters in his belt beneath his coat.

His right thumb pulled the hammer back, then swept up the ambidextrous safety.

With his thumb poised over the safety and his right first finger just inside the trigger guard, but not touching the trigger, Rourke stepped through into the weatherlock, his left hand working the interior flap as Paul, just behind him, told Commander Dodd, "Pull that closed after you, huh?"

Rourke drew open the interior flap.

It was dark inside the tent, only a dull glow of gray daylight lighting the tent walls but providing no illumination at all for the interior.

Rourke's left hand held the German flashlight, his wrists locking together, right over left, the beam from the flashlight and the muzzle of the handgun pointing in the same direction. "Darkwood?"

Paul's voice came from behind him. "John—to your right."

Rourke swung the beam from the flashlight and the gun simultaneously, sidestepping.

The light swept toward one of the cots.

27

On the cot lay the partially clad body of a woman, Maritza Zeiss, her throat slit ear-to-ear, eyes wide open, very little blood across her chest and naked breasts. Blood flow decreased rapidly and coagulation was enhanced under extreme cold. Rourke's breath made steam, the lit cigar in the hand that held the flashlight.

Lying beside her, half on the cot, half off, coat off, pants pulled down to the ankles, lay Jason Darkwood.

"Paul, check the rest of the tent. Dodd, stay with him."

"I'm going for—"

"You're doing just what I say unless you want to get planted right on your ass," Rourke told Dodd emotionlessly, already crossing the tent, dropping to his knees beside Darkwood. There was a dark bruise at the base of Darkwood's skull just at the hairline.

John Rourke felt for a pulse. It was there, a little weak, but he'd felt weaker ones. Breathing was shallow but regular. Darkwood needed treatment quickly, but a few seconds, under the circumstances, wouldn't make that much difference.

Rourke stood, took several steps back, then gradually began moving the flashlight over the two bodies, almost an inch at a time, trying to photograph the scene in his mind. There was a small cut, the blood flow almost negligible, at the left corner of her mouth by the lower lip. A red mark was faintly visible on the left side of her throat, noticeable only because her hair was back, across the pillow, almost arranged that way, it seemed. The red mark appeared to be some sort of abrasion.

The wound itself was a thin line across her throat, either a very sharp knife or something like a straight razor apparently having been used.

Her left nipple was partially torn, but there was no blood visible.

Rourke cursed his stupidity for walking to the tent still smoking the cigar. "Paul? Paul!"

"John?"

"Go over by the bodies and exhale several times, then get as close as you can or you're comfortable with and tell me what you smell."

The younger man nodded grimly. Rourke drew back toward the tent seal, keeping his cigar as far away from Paul as he could.

"It's, ahh—either semen or bleach." Paul Rubenstein stood up.

John Rourke approached the cot again. He shot the flashlight

28

around the tent interior. "Paul. Grab me that inflatable pillow. I don't need the pillow, just the pillow case."

"Right." Paul Rubenstein took the pillow of the next cot, stripped the pillow case from it, handed it to John Rourke. Rourke set down his pistol and flashlight, by the light from Paul's light placing his still gloved hand inside the pillow case, wrapping the pillow case around his hand several times. Slowly, he slid his hand between Darkwood's body and the edge of the cot. Rourke's swathed hand moved over Darkwood's naked abdomen, across the hair at Darkwood's crotch. Then he withdrew his hand.

He held up the pillow case. "Paul. Sniff it. Sorry, the cigar."

Dodd snapped, "I don't have to watch—"

"I agree. Close your eyes," Rourke advised.

"I don't smell it."

Rourke moved his hand back, this time Darkwood's inner thighs. Again, he held up the pillow case. Again, Paul said, "I don't smell it."

Rourke brought the pillow case once more under Darkwood's body, this time along the shaft of the penis and into the area on either side of the testicles.

Even with the cigar, the semen smell was easily detectible. "Smell it now?"

"Yeah," Paul nodded, his eyes darting right and left.

"Give me the plastic inflatable pillow you took this off."

The younger man handed him the pillow. Rourke carefully folded the pillow case to keep the material with the semen sample inside. Now he placed the pillow between Darkwood's genitalia and the edge of the cot, moving the pillow across the penis. When he withdrew the transparent plastic pillow there were small whitish streaks on its surface. "Keep an eye on that."

"All right."

Rourke took up his flashlight again. He searched along the floor. Beside Darkwood's right hand—the fingertips were blood-smeared—was a Mid-Wake issue bayonet. It was blood smeared, too, very likely the murder weapon, regardless of who wielded it. Also on the floor, as if it had fallen from her partially open hand just above it, was a three D-Cell re-chargeable flashlight, of the type in the strategic stores tapped into by the Eden Project personnel. Rourke wasn't concerned about fingerprints.

"Get me another pillow case. Rip this one in half or something so it's easily identifiable."

"Right." In a moment, Paul was back with another pillow case, ripped in half. "What are you going to do?"

"What I have to do," Rourke said hoarsely. Wrapping the pillow case around his hand, he used it to take a semen specimen from the dead woman's genitalia. "Keep an eye on this one, too. We'll get the two specimens typed. Odds are, they match. Then we check that against Darkwood after he provides us with a sample. If Darkwood's sample doesn't match—"

Dodd stammered, "Just a damn minute, Rourke! Just because this man is a friend of yours, you're denying obvious evidence of a rape and murder?"

John Rourke looked over his shoulder at Commander Dodd. "I'm having a hard day. Don't push."

Chapter Six

It was like giving a urine specimen, only worse; and his head ached and his neck ached and when he moved his head his entire body was seized with pain and stiffness. In the end, Jason Darkwood mentally reconstructed an evening more than a year before that he'd spent with Maggie Barrow. Unlike a great many of the officers at Mid-Wake, she had an apartment of her own which she shared with another woman, a Marine Corps officer whose duty schedule was such that she and Maggie rarely even saw one another, one ashore while the other was at sea. Most unmarried Mid-Wake officers, constantly at sea, stayed in available officers quarters when they were ashore.

Maggie had baked lasagna—she was a terrific cook—and there was a bottle of wine and a videotape of some romantic movie from before the war. But they'd only made it about a half-hour into the movie before they'd spontaneously decided to make a romantic tape of their own, but no cameras running.

Making love with Maggie was like nothing he'd ever experienced. She responded to him as if she were a part of him, their hands knowing what to do to each other as if—And then what Darkwood needed to do was done and he felt drained for a moment and there was no sensation of the pain for at least fifteen seconds, but when the pain returned it was more violent than before.

He leaned back in the hospital bed, his face feeling hot, but he took care of the thing.

It wasn't that he hadn't been very tempted with Maritza Zeiss and, maybe, had she lived—He didn't know. Now, he never would.

He rang the nurse call button and, after a moment, the tent of curtain around his bed parted and a German medtech, a young man of about twenty, entered the cubicle. He spoke excellent if somewhat stilted English. "You are finished, Herr Captain Darkwood?"

Jason Darkwood didn't quite know what to say, but nodded, the prophylactic closed at the open end with a rubber band and inside a small beaker of tepid water. It floated around like a communications buoy. "Here."

"The Herr Doctor Rourke would wish to speak with you, Herr Captain."

"Yeah, sure," Darkwood nodded. He shouldn't have nodded. The pain. The German medtech disappeared and, after a moment, there was a knock on one of the support posts for the curtain. "Come in."

It was John Rourke. "Doctor Rourke—"

"Don't stand up, Jason. How are you feeling?"

John Rourke stood beside the bed, his parka absent, his double shoulder holster with his little stainless steel guns visible, worn over a black long sleeved military sweater. "In no special order of importance? Well, stupid, embarrassed, like I'm up shit's creek—was that a real place?—and in a lot of pain."

John Rourke smiled. "I couldn't have you given anything really strong. Because of what you had to do. It's quite important that we have a sample right away. What happened?"

Jason Darkwood shifted position and his head ached all the more, so he fidgeted back. "Okay," and he cleared his throat, a spasm of pain consuming him. "I took her back to her tent, like we agreed. Sure, I thought she was attractive, and maybe I would have tried something with her, but not that way. What's she saying, anyway? I mean, I figured out why you wanted the test."

John Rourke pulled the solitary folding chair around and straddled it as he sat down. "No one's told you, then. She's dead."

Jason Darkwood felt his eyes open wide and the headache worsened instantly. "She's—Now wait a minute."

"What do you remember?"

Darkwood closed his eyes against the pain, and he thought maybe it would help him to remember. He remembered waking up in the hospital bed. He was told he'd been hurt and that it was urgent that he give a sample of ejaculant. He remembered things very fuzzily before that. "I can't tell you."

"Can't?"

"I don't remember, I mean. I took her to her tent and we went inside. Bang. What happened to my head?"

"What do you mean, 'bang'?" Doctor Rourke pressed.

Darkwood shook his head, the pain consuming him. "I, ahh— We went inside and I don't remember anything after that."

"What did you mean earlier when you assumed you suspected the reason we needed an ejaculant sample?"

Darkwood licked his lips. His mouth was very dry. "I assumed something happened and she said I did something to her. I mean, what would you think if you woke up and your head felt ten times too big and somebody wanted you to jerk off into—"

"Were you thinking about her sexually? I mean, at the moment you entered the tent?"

"I don't know. No. I was thinking I was cold. What the hell's going on? What do you mean she's dead? I'm a little slow today, but—"

"Someone murdered Maritza Zeiss and then went to a great deal of trouble to make it appear you'd raped her. The way—"

"I what?" Darkwood sat upright and his head felt as if it would explode and he blinked his eyes against the pain.

Doctor Rourke began again. "The scene, as it appeared, was that you had fought with her, raped her. Her mouth was bleeding. One of her nipples was partially torn off—"

"Oh, God, Doctor—"

"Then, as it was supposed to appear, you slit her throat with a Mid-Wake issue fighting knife—"

"I don't even carry one of those."

Rourke smiled. "I know that you carry a duplicate of a Randall Smithsonian Bowie. Paul knows that, too, as of course do your men, etc. The killer, or whoever put him up to it, didn't. Just as you raked the knife across her throat, with her last ounce of strength she made a valiant effort to kill you, hitting you at the base of the skull with the butt of her flashlight. Evidently, you were supposed to be dead, too. Either the killer was in a hurry or he was either too stupid or too incompetent to tell that you were alive. Your pulse was weak and your breathing was shallow. I tend to think he was in a hurry, which would correspond with another observation, one I made before we came on the scene. There was ejaculant on your—"

"Aww, shit," Darkwood hissed, the pain so intense now he almost didn't care.

"I had the Germans test it. It matches what was found in her vaginal area. The only way to prove your innocence is to compare that to the specimen you just provided us. Unless the killer's your identical twin brother, it won't match. I know you didn't do it; you know you didn't do it. Maritza Zeiss was popular to begin with, a lovely and talented girl and someone the Eden personnel were counting on a great deal, once the weather moderated enough to try crops. That's why you're in the German field hospital, not the one staffed by Eden personnel. There was an attempt at mob justice here once before, under surprisingly similar circumstances, when Natalia was suspected of aiding the Soviets. I didn't want to see history repeat itself."

"What about Sam Aldridge and Lillie St. James and the rest of the Mid-Wake personnel?"

"You mean, do they know about this?" Rourke inquired "Yes. I put them on alert, just in case. Whoever our killer was, he eliminated Doctor Zeiss and tried to eliminate you and, at once, discredit the Mid-Wake officer corps."

"This'll have to be—" Darkwood started, his tongue feeling thick, the pain extremely intense.

"Reported? I'm your C.O., remember? Brigadier General Rourke? Once the lab tests are back, there won't be any charges brought, nothing will go on your record. Your president and your admiral want me to cooperate; well, they can cooperate with me, then. There's a more serious concern than you."

"Oh, I'm glad to hear that."

"I thought you would be, Jason. No, there's a murderer loose and he's working in complicity with Commander Dodd."

"What?" He moved and he shouldn't have.

"That's another reason I wanted you here. I didn't want a mysterious embolism popping up or something. Now, rest."

"Doctor—ah—"

John Rourke reached under his sweater, glanced toward the curtains, then turned the palm of his hand toward Darkwood. In it was Darkwood's own 2418 A2. He'd scratched his initials into the right grip plate years ago. "I can't put it under the pillow. Disrupt hospital routine, and anyway, guns are damned uncomfortable to sleep on. Roll over a little, if you can."

Darkwood rolled over right, felt the mattress being lifted

slightly, then lowered.

"Where'd—"

"Between the mattress and the cot frame. If you need it, you'll have to get out of bed for it. Sorry. But, on the plus side, it's chamber loaded and ready to go. Remind me to see if I can find you a .45. You'd like it better. Trust me."

And John Rourke smiled, then walked out between the curtains. Jason Darkwood lay back. The curtains opened once more. It was Doctor Rourke again. "Trust this medtech. He's one of Colonel Mann's unit. He's got an injection for you. Pain killer. Make you sleep. By the time you wake up, everything should be worked out. Rest well."

The curtains closed, Doctor Rourke vanishing, the medtech approaching the bed. It was the same man who'd taken the sample from him. In his odd but perfectly pronounced English, he said, "It would be better, Herr Captain Darkwood, to administer this injection in your buttocks."

"Just what I needed," Darkwood groaned, rolling over.

Chapter Seven

There were only three still standing modules in what had been the German headquarters complex at their facility outside Eden Base. John had asked that the samples be flown there because Doctor Munchen, the German physician both she and John counted a friend, still had laboratory facilities there, however rudimentary.

Sarah Rourke's eyes narrowed.

John looked through the powerful electronically enhanced microscope. She had just looked through it at the two specimens and seen nothing different between them and that worried her. Jason Darkwood had seemed like such a very nice young man.

John was saying something in medicalese to her, but sometimes he forgot that she had been a nurse and he was a doctor, that she had given up on keeping up with her field after she married him, that he kept up on everything.

He looked at her and, she supposed, realized she wasn't following. "We've got a match."

"Oh, no."

"Relax," her husband smiled. "These are the separate samples I took from Jason Darkwood's genitalia and from Maritza Zeiss."

"Now what?"

Doctor Munchen smiled cheerfully. "Now, Frau Rourke, you can see for yourself that the sample taken from Jason Darkwood does not, in fact, match either of these."

He gestured for her to cross the room again.

She did so, stepping up to the microscope, fingers on the adjustment knobs. "I don't see a difference."

"Touch the button at your left, Frau Rourke," Doctor Munchen advised her. She touched the button. And, suddenly, she saw. As Sarah looked, Munchen continued speaking. The slides were diffused with purple light. "Semen identification techniques have changed little over the centuries, I think. Your husband kindly lent me several books dealing with forensic science. The main difference is the instrumentation with which we are able to examine. A combination of acid phosphatase and ultraviolet light gives us the answers. As you should be able to see, there are subtle differences in the spermatazoa. Fortunate for us, it was so cold that the samples taken from the body of the woman and from the American Captain Jason Darkwood were still viable."

There were subtle differences in shapes, subtle but clearly different.

Sarah looked up from the microscope. "Then this is conclusive proof," she said.

John said, "In two ways. Whoever's semen this matches is the killer, almost unquestionably, unless there were two men, one who did the murder and one who raped her afterward."

Sarah looked at him. "Afterward?"

John nodded.

Munchen said, "The torn nipple. There was no bleeding, which meant, of course, that circulation had stopped, conclusive evidence, of course, that Fraulein Doctor Zeiss was already dead. We have not only a murderer to deal with, but a necrophile as well."

A necrophile was someone who had intercourse with the dead. She shivered.

John's next words made her want to throw up. "Records taken from the leader's private files at New Germany indicate that Freidrich Rausch was into necrophilia. Don't ask for the details. And he's the man whose brother you shot to death, Sarah. He'll be after you."

Someone who raped dead women wanted to kill her. Sarah Rourke shivered again and John folded her into his arms . . .

Christopher Dodd was freezing. He kept walking for two reasons: He had to see Rausch's brother and, if he stopped walking, he might freeze to death.

The sling of the M-16 over his shoulder rattled. It was the only sound amid the silence of the still increasing snowfall except for his own rather labored breathing.

He'd brought the rifle in case some of the KGB people who had escaped the battle might have taken refuge here in the partially constructed permanent base. Certainly, it had been checked, but what if the Russians doubled back?

He reached the foundation and partially erected walls of the community center, snow drifted high as a man's waist in some areas, construction equipment, much of it undamaged despite the attack, all but covered in snow.

"You may stop there, Commander."

Dodd stopped in mid-stride. Damien Rausch had been insane, of course, but there was a certain civility about him, a certain pleasantness when he spoke. Freidrich Rausch had none of these qualities, only the insanity, the ruthlessness, but none of the veneer of humanity.

"May I turn around?"

"You are armed, Commander."

"Yes. I thought there might be Russians about."

"There were three. Trust me. You are safe now."

Dodd slowly started to turn, and, as he did, his eyes saw something red partially covered by a snowdrift in one of the corners made by two unfinished walls.

It was a body, or at least part of one . . .

She lay in their cot and watched him as he cleaned his guns. Sarah Rourke had seen her husband cleaning his little .45s more times than she could remember, but there was something especially meticulous about the way he did it tonight.

She watched him until he was finished. He closed the lubricant—it had a nice enough smell—and walked over to the cot. He placed both pistols on the chair that was beside his side. "I'll have to wash my hands."

Sarah Rourke wondered if that meant he wanted to make love to her. She wanted him to, but her thoughts were still filled with images of Damien Rausch and the body of Maritza Zeiss and she didn't know if she could get those thoughts out of her mind and her heart . . .

* * *

38

Jason Darkwood, in a bathrobe and combat boots, a sweater around his shoulders, sat in the chair beside his bed, his face pale-looking, small lines around his eyes from pain, the eyes slightly glassy-looking with medication. Rourke knew what Darkwood was taking, knew that it would not otherwise dull Darkwood's perceptions.

The only others in the curtained cubicle were Paul, Michael, Sam Aldridge, Wolfgang Mann and Doctor Munchen. Colonel Mann had ordered this segment of the complex of tents which comprised the field hospital cleared of all but those patients who were sedated. His commandoes were posted around the tent.

John Rourke spoke. "We have a very serious problem. In some respects, it's more my problem and Michael's and Paul's than anyone else's; but, in some ways, it's a problem for the German command and the Mid-Wake officer corps. Contrary to the news we released last night, the semen test results were positive, not inconclusive."

Jason Darkwood raised his head.

Rourke continued. "We know that Captain Darkwood is innocent. Granted, we had no doubt of that from the first, those of us who know him, but now there's conclusive proof, the sort of thing that would stand up in a court of law, if need be." Rourke paused for several seconds, rolling his unlit cigar in his fingers. Then, he felt himself smile. "I'm gratified that no one bothered to ask why we let out erroneous information. Because the answer is obvious. As long as Jason Darkwood is considered too weak to provide another sample at this time—the medication for his concussion has induced temporary impotence—"

"Thanks a lot," Darkwood said, his voice strained but a smile on his lips.

Sam Aldridge cleared his throat, sounding as though he were stifling a laugh.

John Rourke went on. "If Captain Darkwood were killed before another sample could be arranged for, Commander Dodd would be in the clear. Crime of passion responsible for the death of the only person who could have conclusively linked Dodd with Damien Rausch, the Nazi conspirator. If murder by a third party is proven, Dodd could be implicated. It would certainly—has certainly—put Commander Dodd under a cloud. Consequently, the real murderer, if we can make things attractive enough for him, will try to rectify his oversight. When the blow was struck to Captain Darkwood's neck, as Doctor Munchen and I agree, evidently the reaction time—" And, now, Rourke looked at Darkwood. "Your reaction time. It was very good. You saved your life without knowing it. When you realized you were being struck, in that split second, you ducked just enough that the blow delivered to you wasn't strong enough to kill. Our killer was very confident, so confident that he never thoroughly checked that you were dead. What we want is for him to attempt to rectify that situation, kill you, Jason."

"Thanks a lot," he nodded again, his eyes showing the strain of his pain.

John Rourke bit down on the end of his cigar. "Doctor Munchen will arrange for certain patients to be transferred to the still standing portions of the hospital at the German base. Jason'll be one of the patients transferred there for extensive recuperation. The other patients, as it were, will be Mid-Wake personnel under the command of Captain Aldridge and some of Colonel Mann's personal commando force.

"The chief physician will be Doctor Munchen," Rourke continued, "but the rest of his staff will be Mid-Wake and German personnel. If we're lucky, the secret will remain a secret and Freidrich Rausch will go for the bait. Then we kill him. Let me reiterate that, gentlemen, since he'll be coming for my wife if he remains alive. We kill him."

Sam Aldridge nodded and whispered, "Amen to that, Doctor Rourke."

"We can't have the place looking more guarded than it should be. I understand that the hurricane in the Gulf is still blowing and reinforcements will be further delayed. In this case, that's to our advantage. We'll have to leave enough people at Eden Base to protect it. That means that proportionately fewer personnel will be available to guard the hospital at what remains of the German base. That makes Freidrich Rausch's chances all the better for success, all the more inviting."

Sam Aldridge asked, "Where's Mrs. Rourke, Doctor?"

"For now, she's under guard by some of Colonel Mann's people, Sam. When this goes down, she'll be far away from here and very safe. Trust that."

"And what about Dodd?" Jason Darkwood sounded very tired, looked it, too.

John Rourke studied his cigar, then looked up. "Unless we take Rausch alive on the assumption that he'll talk—which he wouldn't do voluntarily and we might not be able to get him to do with drugs—there'll likely be no way of making a firm connection between Commander Dodd and the brothers Rausch and the Neo-Nazi movement in New Germany. So, the answer to the obvious question is, no, we won't be able to do anything about Dodd. He's going to have to make a bigger mistake than this. Eden's repopulation for Earth is based on the same system in place at Mid-Wake and, since the overthrow of the leader, in New Germany. In a democratic republic under a system of laws where innocence is presumed until otherwise proven, we don't have a shred of evidence beyond the circumstantial. So, the only way to rid ourselves of Commander Dodd would be to depose him illegally. I don't think we have the right to do that. We can keep pressuring him to hold free elections, but not until the war-footing here has eased a bit. If Eden were to hold free elections today, Akiro Kurinami would undoubtedly be elected president."

"Not to be a wet blanket, Doctor, but Georgia is United States territory. Those space shuttles are United States aircraft. For the past five centuries," Jason Darkwood said, speaking slowly, deliberately, "the government of Mid-Wake has been the government of the United States."

John Rourke shook his head, saying, "You're right, of course, in theory. But the personnel here are not representatives of the United States. They're representatives of every NATO, SEATO and OAS nation, almost every free nation on Earth which ascribed to the same principles as the United States prior to the Night of the War. This is an international community. The government established here won't be a new United States. Granted, Eden Base is on what was once and may still legally be U.S. soil. That'll be something for the government seated at Mid-Wake to work out with Eden Base, but only after Eden Base has a government to negotiate with."

Colonel Wolfgang Mann cleared his throat, inhaling the instant before he spoke. "Back to the subject of Herr Rausch. Should Friedrich Rausch not be apprehended, there is nowhere on earth

41

where Frau Rourke would be safe. I would offer sanctuary in New Germany, but the death of my own wife proved to me that if the Nazis wish to kill someone in New Germany, for the time being at least, they can do so and the forces of law and government are powerless to stop them. Certainly, the assassin might be apprehended, but not until his foul deed is done. What will happen, Herr Doctor, should Rausch not make an attempt on the life of Captain Darkwood? Or, for that matter, should Rausch make such an attempt and make good his escape as well?"

"She'll be safe, Colonel."

"Until?"

Rourke looked at him, smiled. "She'll be safe until Rausch is no longer a threat. I realize The Retreat was discovered by Rausch's brother, penetrated by taking advantage of Kurinami and because of superior numbers. But when Rausch's brother, Damien, died, he was the last of the men to have reached The Retreat. The secret died with him. Aside from a very few persons, persons whom I trust implicitly, the location of and means of entry to The Retreat remains a secret. Sarah will be there, but not alone. I've taken steps that as soon as Major Tiemerovna is well enough to travel from Mid-Wake, both she and my daughter, Paul's wife, will join Sarah at The Retreat.

"We're coming down to it," John Rourke concluded, "to an end to this war, one way or the other. The women have endured enough danger. No more."

Chapter Eight

John Rourke turned on the lights and sluffed out of his parka. The Retreat.

He walked down the three steps to the floor of the Great Room. "I'll get the hot water and everything started," Paul said, leaving his side.

John Rourke only nodded. Paul Rubenstein knew the Retreat's systems as well as he did.

Rourke walked across the Great Room floor, dropping his coat on the arm of the couch. The couch, despite the business with the gunfight between Kurinami and the Neo-Nazis, seemed none the worse for wear. Sarah must have been reading his thoughts, a disturbing idea in light of their daughter's singular abilities. "I was able to repair the bullet holes. Just temporary repairs, but I thought you'd want me to. With all the time I'll have here, I can make a permanent job of it."

"It's a good old couch," Rourke told his wife, sitting down on it on the side nearest the gun cabinets. He could see Paul, just past the kitchen, in the work room, inspecting the motorcycles, the old Harley-Davidson Low Riders. One day, there'd be a time for boarding them again, going out across the land.

He hoped, knew Paul did.

"I'll get you a drink," Sarah said, walking toward the kitchen counter, up the three steps, leaning against it for a moment.

"Are you all right?"

"Just thinking what I'll make for dinner tonight. Can you stay?"

There was no need to consult the Rolex on his left wrist, but out of habit Rourke did so anyway. "I'd like to more than almost anything, but Darkwood will be moved into the hospital at the German Base by now. I have to get back, in case Freidrich Rausch strikes tonight."

43

Sarah was pouring from one of the bottles of whiskey made up for him by the Germans. John Rourke had given them a sample of Seagrams Seven and asked them to duplicate it. They produced one thousand gallons for him. Although the bottles were different, the taste was identical and the supply would last him a lifetime at the modest rate with which he consumed liquor. "You do have time for the drink, don't you?"

"Sure," Rourke told his wife. He noticed she wasn't having one, because of the baby, he knew. He started to get up, but she was already bringing the glass down to him. She handed him the drink and he sipped at the whiskey. "Memories, hmm?"

Sarah smiled, sitting down beside him, but on the edge of the couch. "I'd be all right here by myself until Annie and Natalia and Maria arrive. You might want Paul with you."

Rourke sipped again from his glass, then set it down. "Oh, indeed I would. But I'm not leaving you here alone with Rausch out there. Paul would die for you, just like I would."

Sarah cleared her throat, the sound barely audible. Rourke looked at his wife. "Did it ever occur to you that I'd rather have you live for me, John?"

"What do you mean?"

"I'm tired of war. Sometimes—and understand how I mean this—maybe the ones who died were the lucky ones, the ones who died instantly during the Night of the War."

Rourke took a cigar from his shirt pocket.

Sarah began to speak again. "It's not a death wish. After all we've been through, I'd be an idiot to give it up now. It's not that. Just, I, ahh—I just wish things could be different. I don't want our baby to grow up in a world like this."

John Rourke took out his Zippo.

"I mean, I know we've got great expectations from this new alliance with Mid-Wake, but the Russians aren't just going to lie down and die, either. This thing could go on for decades. It's already been going on for five centuries, John."

Rourke leaned forward and set his cigar and lighter down on the coffee table, then put his left arm around his wife's shoulders. "But it won't. The Russians under the sea have full nuclear capabilities. If we don't stop this war soon, there won't be a planet left to live on. So, it'll all be over, one way or the other, rather soon. Trust me

44

on that. And, if we don't win, at least we'll die knowing we tried. But I think we are going to win. Because we can't let them win. So don't worry, Sarah."

Her body shivered. She leaned her head against his chest. "If there is peace?"

"There's a whole world that's going to need people in it, a world that isn't polluted anymore, isn't overcrowded, doesn't have a drug problem. It could be a good world if we make it that. And, we will. It'd be easy to be a pessimist, but in a strange way the world was given a second chance. And it'll be up to Michael's children and Annie's and Paul's children and the child you're carrying to make that second chance last forever. And they can do it. We just have to keep trying."

"I love you, John Thomas Rourke," Sarah Rourke whispered. John Rourke touched his lips to his wife's forehead . . .

Dinner smelled good, Sarah always a fine cook. He wouldn't be eating it. Rourke told himself there would be other dinners, other times. He smiled as he reflected that he had just summarized the bulk of his married life with Sarah.

Paul stood beside him at the gun cabinets. John Rourke slid back one of the glass doors over the handgun section and took down from a set of wall pegs a gun he'd sent to New Germany with very specific instructions.

"I never had any particular fondness for suppressors, when I was with Central Intelligence or otherwise," Rourke told his friend. "But recently, I've been noticing an occasional need for a more silent shot. Especially with Natalia's Walther being unavailable to us now. And, as much as I'm not the world's greatest admirer of the 9mm Parabellum, there's something to be said for having a large capacity pistol available at times."

"That's a Smith and Wesson, isn't it? But one of the Third Generation guns."

"Yes," Rourke nodded. "It's a 6906." The pistol was about the size of one of Rourke's Detonics mini-guns, brushed stainless steel with the black factory grips.

"The barrel protrudes past the slide for attachment of a silencer, right?"

Rourke smiled. He suddenly remembered the Paul Rubenstein of that day at the wrecked aircraft, not knowing one gun from another as they'd picked through the pile of arms taken from the dead Brigand bikers, arming Paul with the battered old Browning High Power and the German MP-40 submachine gun Paul still regularly carried. Rourke took the suppressor out of a drawer beneath the glassed-in portion of the case. It was black and eight inches long. "You thread it on just like an ordinary barrel extension. Then you lock it into place with an Allen head wrench. The wrench nests in here," Rourke showed him, "in this slot on the side of the unit itself. Just twist and pull it out, use it to tighten the suppressor once it's threaded on, then reinsert it in the side here and twist and the wrench is anchored in place until you need it again to remove the unit. The slide's been fitted with a lock to seal the breach. That's where a lot of the gas escapes and makes noise on pistols which aren't fitted with a lock. I had Colonel Mann's people make me up a batch of subsonic ammunition. The recoil spring was specially modified—the tension reduced—so the pistol would function with the lower energy loads without having to trick up the gun by lightening the slide. They used to do that with movie guns, sometimes, lighten the slide so the action would cycle with blanks. Same idea, basically, but we were able to avoid that. The magazines I have for it all have the feed lips adjusted for the peculiar shape of the bullet itself."

Rourke opened a plain black plastic box, taking from it one of the special subsonic cartridges. The bullet was coated with a black plastic, along the lines of the Nyclad ammunition made by Federal before the Night of the War. But the bullet, although a hollow point, was more truncated and longer than conventional 9mm Parabellums. "Twelve rounds in the magazine. After each shot, if you use the slide lock, work the lock down, cycle the action by hand and raise the lock for the next shot. Without the lock being raised, the pistol functions as it normally would, but of course the noise suppression isn't quite as effective. Depends on the situation in which you're using it."

Rourke set the pistol and suppressor down, then looked at his friend. "When Annie and Natalia and Maria get here, I want you to talk with Annie alone," Rourke told Paul. Rourke's hands were sweating. "If, in her judgement, Natalia's pretty much all right, then do as we planned. Rejoin me. If there's any doubt in Annie's mind about Natalia's stability under the controlled circumstances here, just have the pilot get a message to me or use the radio. But stay put. The Retreat should be as safe as church. That's from the outside. Know what I mean, Paul?"

Paul Rubenstein licked his lips. "Yeah. I don't like leaving them here alone, but I don't want to be sitting back here with four women making me hot meals while you're out there, either, John. But I'll talk with Annie. She's —Natalia, I mean—she's supposed to be all right, or close to it, right?"

"I think so. I pray that she is. I know she wouldn't harm anyone, but she might harm herself. You've gotta be sure, Paul. If you aren't, then don't come. Stay here. Eat those hot meals until you are sure."

The younger man nodded his head. "You know I will."

"Annie should have my note by now." And John Rourke began to pack the pistol, the suppressor, the extra baffle material to refurbish the suppressor, the ammunition. He kept his hands busy so he wouldn't have to speak, the sausage shaped suppressor slick over its anodizing with moisture from his hands . . .

Annie Rourke Rubenstein felt her eyes widen as she unfolded the message. It had been slid under her door while she was away at the hospital visiting Natalia. Natalia seemed stronger, happier every day. She set down her purse. She wondered if she'd ever get used to carrying one on a regular basis. High heels. They made her legs feel good because they made her legs look pretty but they made her feet hurt. She kicked out of them, sinking to the carpeted floor and wiggling her toes. No more did she have her Shore Patrol guardian angels. She traveled Mid-Wake as she pleased. The note in her hands, she crossed the small room and sat on the small window seat, pulling her legs up under her.

"Annie,

"Your mother was forced to kill a man named Damien Rausch during the battle here with the Soviets. Rausch was a Neo-Nazi. Along with a gang of men, he tried killing Akiro at The Retreat. He was the only survivor and, toward the end of the battle, attempted to shoot Akiro in the back. That's when your mom shot him.

"There are some complications, however. Rausch's brother, Freidrich, is thought to be in this area, is the likely killer of one of the Eden Project personnel whom you may or may not have known, Maritza Zeiss—"

Annie remembered her. Very pretty and very smart and very nice. Some day, there'd be a world where she'd sniff back a tear, but she was inured to death, prayed she'd never be used to it. She continued reading her father's radio message.

"—and also attempted to kill Captain Darkwood. Captain Darkwood is doing well. Freidrich Rausch will attempt to kill your mother—"

She dropped the note onto her lap, her hands shaking. She wiped her hands on her gray skirt, picked up the note and read on.

"—unless we can get her to a place of safety. We're doing that until Rausch can be stopped permanently. Paul and I thought—and Paul told me to say he sends his love, as if you didn't know—that your mom would be safer and happier if you and Natalia came to join her. I understand that Natalia's feeling quite a bit better. When you feel that the two of you can join your mom, provided Natalia's willing, notify me through Mid-Wake channels. Admiral Rahn's office will pretty much know where to find me.

"Everyone is well here. Michael's been kind of quiet lately. I think he misses Maria. I'm sending a communique to Maria Leuden, as well, with the same invitation. With four of you ladies in one place, once things settle down, Paul and Michael and I are going to expect a terrific meal, kid. Remember that.

"My love to you, as always, and give my love and Paul's to Natalia as well. Hope to see you soon, honey.

"Love,
"Dad"

Annie stared at the piece of paper, then looked out her window at Mid-Wake's artificial sunshine.

It would be good to be home.

It would be good to be with her mother and Michael's girl, Maria.

But would it be good for Natalia?

She looked at the artificial sunlight for a while.

All of the old problems which had caused Natalia to become ill in the first place still existed. The fantasy that Natalia's dead husband, Vladmir Karamatsov, still somehow lived might never more haunt Natalia. But there were real things enough to drive her back, over the edge from reason.

More than ever, she knew that Natalia loved her father, John Rourke.

But it was a love that could never be fulfilled because her father was faithful to her mother. It was as simple as that, on the outside looking in (as she had done). Annie tried to imagine a life where she was in love with Paul, as she always had been, but could not be his.

It would be hell.

Natalia lived there.

Chapter Nine

John Rourke gave the suppressor a good luck twist, then removed the Allen wrench from the body of the suppressor and began tightening the suppressor to the Smith and Wesson 6906's extended barrel.

"That's a neat gun, Doctor," Sam Aldridge said, touching up the edge of his Ka-Bar-like Marine Corps knife on what passed these days for ceramic sharpening sticks.

They sat in the German Base hospital's lounge area, an ordinary waiting room with a moderately comfortable couch and two chairs, a video player and several magazines, the magazines and the few videos from New Germany. Except for the language in which the magazines were written and the video player—a combination tape machine and television set that was a bottom feed unit and only a few inches thick, hung on the wall like a framed picture—the room was timeless.

The waiting room was the ready room for persons on guard at the German base's hospital or those supervising the guard details. John Rourke began loading a twelve-round magazine for the suppressor-fitted 6906, every few rounds thwacking the spine of the magazine against his palm to more properly seat the cartridges.

"What are you gonna use that for, Doctor Rourke?"

Rourke looked across the low table at Sam Aldridge. "I'm not sure, Sam. But when I eventually need it, I'll have it." The magazine loaded, he inserted it up the butt of the pistol; then, verifying that the hammer drop safety was lowered, he worked the slide. One other modification to the little pistol about which he had neglected to tell Paul Rubenstein was the deletion of the magazine safety. A magazine safety on a pistol, Rourke had always thought, was just as practical and potentially useful (and as fraught with hazard) as a screen door on the hatch of one of Mid-Wake's submarine fleet.

"That a Colt?"

Rourke smiled. "It's a Smith and Wesson."

"I thought they made revolvers, like the one you carry."

"Well, they made these things, too," Rourke answered patiently. "The barrel and the suppressor are sort of aftermarket items."

"Think Rausch'll come tonight?"

"Jason's set, got his pistol within reach. We've got men outside, men inside. If Rausch comes, he'll have to be damned good to get away."

"I mean Jason, Doctor. Is there any chance—"

"I know Jason's your best friend, Sam. Sure there's a chance. But Darkwood knows that. There wasn't any other choice. Rausch won't want to leave Darkwood hanging around to implicate Dodd, because, evidently, he needs Dodd. The Nazis require a base of operations, supply, like that. Lieutenant Kurinami discovered that the master computer files aboard the command shuttle were wiped clean; all the locations of the strategic stores laid away for the Eden Project on its return were on those files. But Kurinami duplicated them. Logic dictates that Dodd copied them before wiping them away. Kurinami being possessed of a duplicate set means Dodd doesn't have all the power. I sent Kurinami to the front with Captain Hartmann's men. Hartmann is Colonel Mann's field commander for the forces covering the Soviet Underground City. Hartmann's a good officer. I offered that Akiro and Elaine could go into hiding. He wouldn't. There was a war to be fought, he said. Kurinami's that kind of guy. Elaine wanted to stay here. She wouldn't stay with my wife and daughter because if Akiro was going to stay in the thick of things, she had to, too. I talked her into going to Mid-Wake, at least, to help with the war effort there where her scientific background could be of some assistance. And she should be safe there. Both of their attitudes are admirable, but short-sighted under the circumstances. If Dodd can kill Kurinami, or use Elaine to get to him, Dodd will have obliterated any chance for the restoration of the computer files, except by himself. That's why Dodd's playing footsie with the Nazis. As long as there's a war on with the Soviets, he doesn't have to worry about the Soviets supplying Eden, certainly. If he can disrupt New Germany, maybe Dieter Bern and Colonel Mann's people won't be able to help

51

much, either. I doubt he cares much for Mid-Wake. Dodd wants to be the only source of help to Eden, so he can control it."

Aldridge put down his knife. "Isn't it kinda dangerous, Doctor, I mean with the Japanese guy? He could get K.I.A.ed and the files would be lost."

"No they wouldn't be," John Rourke smiled. "You see—" As he began to elaborate, there was a sound in the corridor just beyond the door. Rourke was up, the Smith and Wesson autopistol shoved into the small of his back into the waistband of his black BDUs. His fists closed over the two Scoremasters, snatching them up from the table, stuffing them into his waistband on either side of his abdomen. His left hand caught up first his flashlight and then the M-16 he'd left by the door, his right hand moving to the door-knob.

He heard the rattle of the sling from Aldridge's Soviet AKM-96, originally picked up off the battlefield after the Soviets were forced back in the aftermath of the attack on Eden. Rourke had noticed a number of the Marines doing the same, preferring it to their issue rifle. It seemed to be a better gun, Rourke had to admit.

Rourke stepped into the corridor, a shaft of light washing over the floor from behind him.

There was no one visible.

"What was it, you think?"

Rourke didn't look at Aldridge as he spoke. "Probably nothing; just our nerves. You check the guards on Darkwood. I'll check by the entrance."

Rourke started moving, running in a long-strided, almost easy, loping gait, the M-16 in his right fist by the pistol grip, in his left the communicator. "This is Rourke. Guard stations, come back to me in sequence."

Guard stations one, two, three and four reported. There was nothing from guard station five, near the loading dock where non-ambulatory patients were brought in for treatment or removed for a flight to better hospital facilities in New Germany. "Guard station six, come in."

Guard station six came back.

John Rourke quickened his pace, changing frequencies so he could contact Aldridge as he did. "This is Rourke. Do you read me, Aldridge? Over."

Aldridge's voice crackled back. "Loud and clear, Doctor. No problems, here. Over."

"Guard post five on the interior perimeter is not responding. I'm checking it now. Stay alert. Out."

Rourke reached the farthest edge of the perimeter for the remaining modules of the hospital. It was darker here in the corridor and, despite the insulation, cold enough that, as he exhaled, he could see his breath, like small patches of fog in a night intermittently lit by a sliver of moon, various shafts of lights from the corridors and medical facility rooms he passed providing the only illumination.

He carried a flashlight in his belt and, merely by using the radio, could have contacted one of Aldridge's men or one of the Germans to flick on every light in the building. But he stayed in the semi-darkness, his eyes accustoming to it quickly, his light sensitivity a benefit to him at times like these.

There was a blizzard surrounding them. Conditions had made it nearly impossible to reach the German base after leaving the Retreat, the high winds which whipped the snow a side effect of the fizzling hurricane in the Gulf. And the wind gnawed through pin-hole size apertures and cracks between modular wall segments and roofing here, the sound like a hundred banshees moaning in low whispers from cold, uneasy graves.

He passed guard post three, the German Commando and the American Marine there, alert, ready for anything.

Rourke kept moving, toward the glow of light from guard post four.

It was the same there, the American and the German on duty, all as it should be.

Guard post five was located near the wards, and to have used his assault rifle near even such a small concentration of people would have been unconscionable madness, the 5.56mm round it fired too penetrative for safe employment.

He slung the M-16 across his back, left shoulder to right hip, muzzle down.

He was better armed for close combat than he had ever been in his life, and close combat it might well be. On the outside of his belt at the small of his back in the Rybka M.O.B. holster was the old two-inch barreled Colt Lawman MkIII .357 Magnum revolver, the Lawman loaded with 125-grain jacketed hollow point .357s. At his right hip was the Smith 629, at his left hip the LS-X knife. The little Detonics pistols were holstered beneath his battered brown bomber jacket in the double Alessi shoulder rig he always used with them. The full-sized Scoremasters were in his belt, the A.G. Russell Sting IA Black Chrome hidden inside the waistband of his trousers as well, but at his back.

None of these was the right choice here.

John Rourke drew the suppressed 6906, offing the safety as he moved out of the light of guard post four.

The subsonic bullet would be less penetrative than any other round available to him and silence might prove an advantage. His fingers checked the slide lock. It was lowered and he left it that way. Not that much silence would be needed, and fast follow up shots could be important.

He kept going, keeping his pace slow, even, as he walked into the darkness. And he realized he was afraid. There was always some personal fear in battle; men who denied experiencing it were either liars or lunatics. But it was not this sort of fear, now, which gripped him deep in the pit of his stomach, made his hands slightly slick. If something should go wrong and he should miss this chance, then Rausch would be alive to attempt to kill Sarah, kill Darkwood, aid Commander Dodd in his efforts to turn Eden Base into his personal fiefdom.

None of that could be allowed to happen.

John Rourke stopped walking, nearing guard post five, near enough that he should have seen their light. There was none to see.

He moved closer to the corridor wall, the whistling moans of the wind from the storm surrounding the German base hospital more intense, or his awareness of the sounds more acute. He couldn't be sure which.

His back to the wall, John Rourke edged forward, keeping his pistol close at his side, his eyes slightly averted lest Rausch should attempt to momentarily blind him with high intensity light.

From the darkness ahead of him, he heard a voice. "Herr Doctor. Do not move!"

Rourke froze, his right fist locked on the butt of the suppressor-fitted 6906.

The voice again. "I am Freidrich Rausch, Herr Doctor. I have come to kill your meddlesome friend, Captain Darkwood. Consider the Herr Captain's death merely a prelude, an overture to the death of your wife. I will find her, kill her."

"Try killing me, mother fucker," Rourke hissed, dropping to a crouch so deep he was nearly on his knees. Unless Rausch wore vision intensification glasses, there was no way Rausch could clearly see him, Rourke realized.

"I will kill you, indeed, but only after a most unpleasant murdering of your wife. Sarah is her name, is it not? Death is so much less profoundly felt without mourning; would you not agree?" John Rourke feared for his wife, and he'd experienced fear before, hoped to live to experience it again. But he had never been paralyzed by it. While Freidrich Rausch talked, John Rourke moved.

He edged back along the corridor, toward the nearest open doorway, literally diving across the corridor from one side to the other and through the doorway, coming up out of a roll onto his knees. His back hurt him slightly because of the unnatural way he had moved to avoid the rifle slung there scratching across or banging into the floor and making a betraying noise.

He was up, to his feet, telling himself the muscle pains would work themselves out and, as he moved, they were.

Because of the modular construction of the base hospital, each block of rooms was designed to connect in a variety of ways to similar or dissimilar blocks for maximum utility; hence, there were interconnecting doors and demountable walls.

John Rourke moved quickly to the first door, tried it, opened it, his right fist tight on the butt of the suppressor-fitted 6906.

The door opened onto one of the wards, a half dozen actual German casualties here. As Rourke passed by the nearest bed, he nearly slipped.

Rourke took the battered Zippo windlighter from his BDU pocket and cupped his hands around it as he rolled the striking wheel under his thumb. He had nearly slipped in a pool of blood. The man in the bed had a throat that was slit almost literally from ear to ear.

Rourke slowly, soundlessly closed the cowling of the Zippo, extinguishing the blue yellow flame, his eyes still seeing it as an after image as he checked the next occupied bed. Here, too, the man was murdered.

55

The others would be the same, Rourke realized.

"Herr Doctor? How does it feel to be so totally helpless to prevent the death of your wife?"

Rausch's voice talking from the corridor or near to it.

Rourke kept moving, across the floor of the ward toward the demountable wall, ramming the 6906 into his belt for an instant as his hands found the locking mechanism, worked it—there were squeaking sounds—and unlocked the wall from its frame. Rourke drew the sliding accordion panel back just enough that he could pass through.

But he cautiously looked beyond the demountable wall first, because Freidrich Rausch had stopped talking.

Chapter Ten

Jason Darkwood sat up on the edge of his bed, wondering if he should lie down again. Would he make a more inviting target, lying back in his bed? More helpless? More easy prey for this man who killed people in the name of a doctrine at the mention of which sane men were disgusted, filled with revulsion?

But he could not lie back.

He sat there, instead, his left hand beside his pillow, beneath his pillow both the Lancer 2418 A2 semi-automatic pistol and his knife. On a practical level, he took great comfort from the gun, a weapon with which he could shoot bullseyes all day long at twenty-five yards, a weapon he had carried in combat ever since his first days out of the Academy. Officers could purchase the issue pistol, if they wished, and he had very soon purchased his. His second paycheck, he suddenly remembered. The first one he owed most of to two friends who'd lent him money. By the third paycheck, he was mercifully at sea and there was no need to spend money for billeting or food.

There'd been times when money was tight in those early days, until he'd learned to manage it; but the gun had always stayed with him.

Yet, somehow, he took greater comfort from his knife. It was an identical duplicate, down to the metallurgy, of the Randall Smithsonian Bowie his ancestor had brought to Mid-Wake.

It had heritage.

And, it was personal.

It would be useless at twenty-five yards. But Freidrich Rausch would not come from twenty-five yards.

Rausch would be close when and if Rausch came.

Darkwood's palms perspired. He waited.

When Sam Aldridge had said, "I'll be back later, Jason; gonna check around some more," Darkwood had been desirous of telling him, "Hey, Sam—don't leave me alone here, huh? I'm spooked." But, instead, he'd told his friend, "I'm fine. Let me know how things are going, okay?"

And Sam Aldridge had gone.

Now Jason Darkwood waited alone in the darkness.

Chapter Eleven

John Rourke was beside the corridor wall, behind him a patient lounge. His hearing, always excellent despite his exposure over the years to so much gunfire without the benefit of hearing protection, enabled him now to almost pinpoint the origin of Rausch's voice. This worried him. Why was Rausch being so careless?

A thought crossed John Rourke's mind, and the thought chilled him.

Cautiously, the pistol in his right fist, John Rourke reached out to touch his fingertips to the door handle. But, instead, he drew his hand back. Again, he thrust the pistol into his belt and took the Zippo from his pocket. The flashlight would have been easier to use but easier to spot from the other side of the doorway as well. Rourke shielded the lighter with his body to muffle any noise of striking flame, then dropped to a crouch beside the doorway, moving the lighter close to the handle. Leading out of the handle's base were two thin pieces of wire. Turning the door handle would bridge the wires. Rourke's lighter and his eyes followed the wires down to the base of the door, then along the base molding and along the wall. The wires ended at the wall outlet.

If he had opened the door without thinking, he would have electrocuted himself.

John Rourke felt a smile cross his face. Rausch had re-taught him a valuable lesson: And that was never to underestimate an enemy.

John Rourke unsheathed the LS-X knife and went to work on the wires.

Chapter Twelve

Jason Darkwood lay back in the bed, telling himself he had not heard a noise, that nothing was going to happen. There were two United States Marines on duty at the end of the hall and all of the connecting doors were blocked and locked.

He could hear the wind, his room on an outside wall of the central courtyard for the hospital. Doctor Munchen had explained to him, "We have always felt that psychological well-being is a great contributor to physical well-being. Often, a chance to experience the sunlight, the fresh air, a pleasant breeze, can be quite surprisingly therapeutic. With the modular construction of our field hospitals, it is very simple to merely leave out a center module, or even several, thus creating a central courtyard in which recuperating patients can experience a natural environment. Statistics indicate as high as a five percent reduction in overall hospitalization in hospitals using this technique, among a certain class of patients, of course. I feel its validity can best be tested against the opposite extreme. Here, in American Georgia as of late, the climate is so extreme that patients, no matter how otherwise hardy, cannot be exposed to the cold and the snow. Periods of hospitalization, based on preliminary raw data, with comparative wounds to comparative personnel, are of greater duration. But perhaps the snow will stop."

This was Darkwood's first truly prolonged experience on the surface, and the weather astounded him in its severity. That men constantly lived and worked and fought with such conditions of extreme cold, high winds and falling snows was a testimony to their character and their endurance.

Darkwood felt himself smile. He imagined a surface dweller would have marvelled equally at the adaptability shown by Mid-Wake personnel to a life—How could he classify the life of Mid-Wake? Enclosure? One was almost always enclosed, beneath the

60

great domes of Mid-Wake itself, within the hull of one of Mid-Wakes vessels. Only a very few were ever able to escape enclosure, albeit for a brief period of time. Even swimming as part of a mission rarely took someone to the surface; and, while swimming, one wore helmet and suit and was encased from head to toe, even the hands.

Suddenly, Jason Darkwood wanted to be in the cold, feel the wind, the snow.

He stood up—a little too quickly—and held onto his nightstand.

Here he was a prisoner, really, enclosed within the walls of this room, within the larger confines of the building itself. There was a door leading to the outside. But logic dictated he not pass through it.

Prisoners of ice and snow and wind and prisoners of the sea were very much alike.

There was a sound, like something scratching against the outer door leading to the courtyard. It wasn't like any of the sounds he had heard before, the howling of the wind, the creaking of the very building joints themselves at times.

Darkwood took up his pistol, stared at it.

Was it Rausch come to get him?

His right fist tightened on the butt of the Lancer 2418 A2. He wished he had some sort of missile at his command instead of just a pistol.

Jason Darkwood edged back from the door to the outside, crossing the room toward the door leading to the corridor. Was it merely the fact that it was "outside" beyond that door which somehow, on an almost primordial level, terrified him?

He had his hand reaching out for the door handle leading to the corridor, to an inside place, enclosed.

Darkwood stopped moving his hand.

If he touched that door handle, he would be giving in to the fear which had begun to grip him here, stalked by Rausch, trapped in an unfamiliar environment, one of unbridled hostility, his head and neck aching, medication for the pain coursing through his system.

Darkwood thrust his left hand into the pocket of his robe so he couldn't reach for the door handle. He knew enough about the human body to know that things like fear and confidence were controlled by chemical triggers. Some chemical trigger—it had to

61

be the medication—was tying him in knots of indecision. But he could start other chemical triggers working. Brave men conquered their fear because they had no choice, not because they wanted to. He had no choice.

Jason Darkwood started walking—slowly because he couldn't walk rapidly—toward the door to the outside. If Freidrich Rausch were waiting for him, then the thing would get over with quickly, one way or the other.

Darkwood gripped the pistol tighter.

Chapter Thirteen

It was a tape player, not modern like those of new Germany, but state-of-the-art for the era of John Rourke's earlier life in the Twentieth Century. It was from one of the Eden Project supply caches.

"You must know, Herr Doctor, that you cannot win. Ours is an historic struggle. I have calculated your actual chronological age to arrive at the date of your birth. What a pity! I feel terrible sorrow for you that you were born only after the great hero of humanity was sacrificed on the altar of mediocrity as a sacrifice to the demagogues of the self-styled democracies. To have lived in those days when Der Fuhrer walked the earth like mortal man and to have breathed air that might have touched him—"

John Rourke pushed the button for stop and the tape machine clicked off.

Freidrich Rausch had been smarter than John Rourke's reappraisal of the man's capabilities had even suggested. Somewhere along the corridor, there would be a photo-electric eye or pressure sensitive strip. John Rourke's having passed through or on whatever it was had activated the tape recorder's play mechanism. Rausch had intentionally come here, to the most remote of the interior perimeter outposts. And killed.

Near Rourke's feet, as he shone the light, were two bodies, throats slashed ear to ear, one body that of an American Marine from Mid-Wake, the other that of a commando of New Germany.

John Thomas Rourke took the cassette from the recorder. Something—some random sound in the background—anything might prove of some use.

And he ran.

Because Freidrich Rausch would be at the heart of the hospital complex, ready to kill Jason Darkwood, if Darkwood weren't dead already . . .

Jason Darkwood's head ached with the movement. Doctor Munchen had told him to expect some pain, even some disorientation under mental or physical stress. The blow to his head had been severe. He was feeling vaguely nauseated.

Darkwood's palms sweated. Pain. Disorientation. Yes. He had both. And there was a chemical reaction going on in his body that was making things very bad for him.

He touched his left hand to the locking bolt on the door leading to the outside, to the snow-drifted courtyard.

He slid the bolt back.

His left hand gripped the door handle, his right fist tightening on the butt of the 2418 A2.

"Open the door," Darkwood told himself. "It's only a door. It'll be a little cold. That's all right. Anything out there, hey, no problems. I blow it away with this." He held the pistol close by his right side. He wished he had one of the thirty-round magazines in it instead of only a fifteen. Then he would have had thirty-one shots instead of only sixteen.

He didn't.

He twisted the door handle.

The door was stuck.

Darkwood tugged at it, a cold sweat breaking out over his kidneys, under his armpits, dizziness sweeping over him. He pulled harder and the door opened, an icy wind almost knocking him down, swirling around inside his hospital room like the terrestrial whirlwinds he had studied about in geography and climatology classes when he was a boy in school.

He shivered. "The wind," Darkwood murmured.

Snow was drifted several feet high beside where the door had been and it formed a flange there now, at the base and on the left hand side of the doorframe as well, sculpted flat and smooth, grainy, textured too.

"Anybody out there?"

Only the wind replied . . .

John Rourke reached the center corridor running as he spoke into the walkie-talkie. "He can hear us, Sam, hear us, I'd lay money on it. He can hear every word we say. He's closing in on Darkwood right now, if he hasn't gotten him already."

"My two Marines—that mother fucker. They're not answering!"

"Dead. One Marine and one German Commando dead on post five and probably more between there and Darkwood's room. He's good. He's so good he's scarey. We're gonna get him. Hear that, Rausch? We're gonna nail your ass."

Rourke could hear Sam Aldridge's breathing as Aldridge opened the frequency again. Aldridge was running . . .

Jason Darkwood stood in the doorway's threshold, his left hand balled into a fist to keep his robe closed at his throat, his entire body trembling with cold and the dizzy feeling in his head. He called into the swirling snow and the darkness beyond the meager cone of white light from the doorway, his form silhouetted in it. "I know you're out there. You want to kill me, then come ahead, you shit!"

Darkwood stepped through the doorway . . .

John Rourke had planned ahead.

If Freidrich Rausch had access to one tape recorder, he had equal access to many. If Freidrich Rausch realized that the first tape recorder would be discovered, he might assume that no one would in turn assume he would utilize a second tape recorder in the same way as the first, to draw someone to it, but this time for a totally different purpose.

John Rourke punched through the doorway into the vacant patient room across the central courtyard and opposite from the identical quarters occupied by Jason Darkwood.

Rourke ran to the window, pushed back the curtain. Jason Darkwood stood in the snow, just outside the open doorway leading from his room, shaky looking. It could be a reaction of adrenaline with the medication Doctor Munchen had administered to aid in Darkwood's recovery.

And at the edge of the shaft of light flooding over the snow through the open doorway, inside the room, behind Darkwood, there was the figure of a man.

John Rourke couldn't risk a shot.

Rourke looked to his right, the sliding hospital bed table so much like those used five centuries ago the nearest heavy object to hand. He grabbed it, wresting it free of the bed with his right hand as his left hand reached out for the door handle. He could hurtle the table through the open doorway into the courtyard and distract—

Rourke almost touched the door handle.

The flashlight from his belt. He grabbed it, letting the table rest against the wall.

Rourke dropped to a crouch beside the door handle, in the beam of the flashlight seeing the wires, the same as before, an obvious invitation to cut them. But, tracing them to the nearest outlet, Rourke saw another set of wires, the first set a blind. As he moved, his right foot slipped a little and as he shone the flash over the floor he detected a puddle of water, a wire set in its center. He followed the second collection of wires back toward the door handle; if he'd cut the first and obvious set, the second set would have gotten him.

John Rourke was out of time. He shoved the flashlight into his belt as he raised to his full height and swung the M-16 forward on its sling.

He could see Darkwood starting to turn around as the shadow of the man who stalked him obscured a portion of the shaft of light in which Darkwood stood.

John Rourke fired the M-16 through the synthetic transparent panel which served as a window to the courtyard, blowing it out in huge jagged chunks, spraying the 5.56mm bullets across the base into which the glass-substitute was set so he could scramble through without ripping his clothing and the flesh beneath it to shreds. Darkwood was already wheeling toward the sound of gunfire, but not toward the shadow.

The M-16 empty, John Rourke let it fall to his right side on its sling, his right hand grasping for the butt of the six-inch barreled .44 Magnum revolver at his right hip.

He drew, starting the trigger squeeze as his right arm raised to shoulder height and his left palm cupped around his right fist.

The figure stepped out of the shadow, fully backlit now, a sinister silhouette with some sort of crossbow shouldered and ready to fire.

The figure—it had to be Rausch—ducked left as Darkwood, apparently alerted by some sound or some movement, turned toward him. Perhaps the sound of the crossbow's safety catch being flicked off, Rourke thought.

Rourke's revolver discharged, the crossbow flying from the figure's right hand, the figure falling back.

Rourke's shot missed the intended target, the silhouetted figure's center of mass.

Darkwood fired his pistol, the muzzle flash—lower with the caseless ammunition than with conventional gunpowders—a quick tongue of flame that endured for only an instant. There was an answering flash from inside the room and Darkwood stumbled back, fell into the snow as John Rourke vaulted through the shot out window and into the courtyard.

Darkwood was up on his elbow, firing the pistol again as Rourke reached him. "It was Rausch! Had to be!"

John Rourke heard the slamming of a door from inside.

"Get inside if you can. I'll send help!" Rourke grabbed for his walkie-talkie. "Sam! This is Rourke. Rausch is in the corridor outside Darkwood's room. Rausch tried and missed. He's armed. Get help to Darkwood."

He didn't wait for an answer, hitting the doorway into the room, his clothes wet with snow from the brief seconds outside in the courtyard, the 629 in his right fist.

Rourke crossed the room in two long strides, grabbed up a chair from near the bed, returned to the open doorway and threw the chair through into the corridor.

A burst of automatic weapons fire tore through the seat back, almost severing the chair in two before it hit the corridor floor.

Rourke stabbed the 629 through the doorway and emptied the remaining five rounds from the cylinder in the direction from which the gunfire had originated. He dropped the 629 into the Sparks holster and drew both Detonics Scoremasters, thumbing back the hammers as he went through the doorway, firing both pistols simultaneously, crossing the corridor to the doorway opposite but slightly nearer the origin of the gunfire, chunks of wall and doorframe spraying around him, Rourke's eyes squinting against the cloud of debris.

There was something in his right eye. He blinked both eyes as he looked down at his pistols, both pistols still holding four rounds each. Backing deeper into the doorway, blinking his eyes to clear the right one, Rourke stabbed both pistols toward Rausch's position, firing them out, another hail of automatic weapons fire tearing into the doorframe.

Rourke thrust both pistols into his belt, the slides still locked open over the empty magazines. His right hand found the butt of the Colt Lawman at the small of his back, drawing it from the Rybka M.O.B. holster, punching the snubby .357 Magnum blindly down the corridor, firing as his left hand rolled back his right eyelid. Involuntary paroxysms traveled up his spine as he touched his left index finger to his eyeball. Rourke shrank from his own hand, the revolver empty. He blinked his eye, tears rolling from it.

The offending bit of building material was gone.

Rourke grabbed for his flashlight, flicking it on, staring into the light with his right eye, making the tears come more freely now. More gunfire. Rourke stuffed the Lawman into the right hip pocket of the black BDU pants he wore, shaking his head, both hands reaching for the little Detonics Combat Masters under his armpits, ripping the miniaturized stainless steel .45s from the double Alessi rig.

His thumbs jacked back the hammers and he punched both pistols around the doorframe simultaneously, firing a double tap from each.

More automatic weapons fire, the sound light enough to be a 9mm submachine gun.

Rourke shifted the pistol in his right hand to his left, both of the little .45s held uselessly there for a moment as he pulled the magazine from the M-16, stuffed the empty into a front pocket, then snatched a fresh thirty-round spare from his musette bag.

He rammed it home, pressuring his hip against the wall to lock the rifle in place as his right hand worked the bolt, jacking a round into the chamber.

Rourke shifted one of the little Combat Masters back to his right hand, firing both pistols out, keeping them in the open a split second too long so that Rausch would realize they were empty.

A long burst of automatic weapons fire into the doorframe and wall.

Again, John Rourke had planned ahead. Rausch would have assumed no rational man, facing an opponent armed with an automatic weapon, would respond with pistol fire if he had another option.

As Rourke shifted the Detonics Combat Master from his right hand to his left, his right fist found, then closed over the M-16's pistol grip, thrusting the Colt assault rifle outward, tensioning it against the sling. Rourke stepped into the corridor, Freidrich Rausch just disappearing around a bend at its far end. Rourke fired, taking a chunk out of the corner of the corridor, Rausch staggering for a split second before he ran on.

John Rourke ran after him.

Chapter Fourteen

Jason Darkwood raised the leg of the hospital bed, kicking the inverted kidney shaped bedpan in place beneath it.

He dropped to his knees, shaking with fear.

If adrenaline had done it to him, reacted chemically with the medication Doctor Munchen had prescribed, then more adrenaline would undo it—he hoped.

He inserted a fresh magazine up the well of the 9mm Lancer Caseless, put the fingers of his left hand beside the bedpan, closed his eyes and rammed the edge of his hand against the bedpan, knocking it away, letting the leg of the bed crash down on his fingers.

Jason Darkwood almost screamed with the pain, sprawling back, his hand still trapped beneath the leg of the bed.

He shook his head.

The adrenaline rush came.

He could feel the nausea replaced with pain.

To his knees. He threw his body weight against the bed frame as he lifted up with his right hand, freeing his left hand.

His fingers didn't move.

He didn't care.

Darkwood reached out for his pistol, his knife already sheathed, his pistol belt around his waist.

To his feet.

He stumbled, nearly collapsing over his bed, the pain so intense that the nausea was returning to him. But the fear, the fear which had slowed his reflexes, dulled his senses, nearly paralyzed him— the fear was gone.

Jason Darkwood started for the door, his throbbing left hand useless at his side, his right fist tight on the butt of the 2418 Al.

Chapter Fifteen

John Rourke reached the bend in the corridor, the M-16 extended ahead of him like a magic wand against death. "It's me! Rourke! Shout or I'll shoot!" There was no answering call from Sam Aldridge or any of the Germans or the U.S. Marines. The M-16 still tight in his right fist, he shouted again. "Aldridge?" No answer. Wrist bent, Rourke stabbed the assault rifle around the corner and fired out two three-round bursts in rapid succession.

He tucked back, letting the M-16 fall to his side on its sling, putting fresh magazines as rapidly as he could up the wells of the Detonics .45s, Combat Masters and Scoremasters.

He fired out the M-16, made a fast tactical change and dodged into the corridor for an instant, pulling back.

No sign of Rausch.

"Shit," Rourke hissed.

He looked to the wall opposite him. It was an empty patient room, the kind reserved for an officer or senior non-com with two beds only, the type Darkwood occupied. But no one occupied it now.

John Rourke grasped the M-16 in both fists and fired, starting from the floor up, zig-zagging the muzzle as he controlled the long, magazine-emptying burst, cutting a rough shape in the wall near to his own size. He pulled back, letting the rifle fall to his side, the metal of the barrel by now hot enough to burn.

A Scoremaster in each hand, Rourke threw himself against the wall, left shoulder first, his body momentum crashing through the cutout portion of the wall, crumbling beneath his weight as he stormed through, falling to his knees, eyes closed against the dust and debris, his eyes opening, only partially, on his knees, a pistol still locked in each hand.

There was a door on the far side of the room.

Rourke scrambled up from his knees and ran for it. He stopped before the door, took a half step back, pivoted on his right foot and made a double Tae-Kwon-Do kick at the handle, the door shattering open outward. There was gunfire from the right. Rourke drew back, his walkie-talkie picking up Sam Aldridge's voice. "Doctor, where are you?"

Rourke looked into the corridor, able to make out the number on the crumbled, now bullet riddled door. "By patient room six after the bend in the corridor and up from the corridor leading off Darkwood's room. Over."

"I'm at Jason's room now. He's with us. Ready to fight. Sounds like a machine gun or something down there. Over."

"Close from Darkwood's room to the bend in the corridor, take the right carefully and we'll have Rausch between us. And he's got a submachine gun of some sort. Rausch—you hear that? Got you trapped! Rourke Out."

Rourke fired both pistols around the frame of the doorway. Answering fire came, ripping out chunks of the doorframe as Rourke tucked back. Had Rausch been firing a machine gun, as Aldridge had labelled it, hiding behind the relatively flimsy construction of the hospital room doorframe as Rourke did now wouldn't have been just dangerous, it would have been insane. But the concept of a submachine gun was almost militarily unknown at Mid-Wake, the assault rifle or the high capacity pistol taking its place.

He safed both pistols and thrust them into his belt, then put a fresh magazine up the well of the M-16. There was another burst of submachine gun fire. Rourke punched the M-16 around the corner of the doorframe in his left fist and fired, turreting the gun right and left and right, drawing back as answering fire came back.

If he could provoke Rausch into firing out his submachine gun, while Rausch made the tactical magazine change, he—Rourke— could cross the corridor and advance into the doorway of the patient room just up the corridor. The popular misconception of the term 'machine gun' had always amused him, yet simultaneously saddened him in the ignorance it reflected. Rausch had a submachine gun, an automatic or selective fire weapon which fired a pistol-sized caliber, a sub-caliber as opposed to the rifle calibers used in machine guns, hence the designation "submachine gun." Rourke remembered reading in newspapers and magazines, or hearing television newsbroadcasters solemnly proclaim that "machine gun wielding terrorists—"

Rourke had always marveled at how muscular the subject terrorists or robbers or whatever they were would have had to be, since holding something like an M-60 machine gun and firing it at the same time required considerable physical strength.

Ignorance worked many miracles otherwise impossible in the real world.

Rourke punched the M-16 around the doorway again, snapped off a quick burst, drew back, an answering fusillade of submachine gun fire, Rourke firing back, emptying the magazine, a long burst of submachine gun fire and nothing for an instant.

John Rourke let the emptied M-16 fall to his side on its sling as he threw himself through the doorway into the corridor, both Scoremasters blazing in his fists. The doorway. Rourke dove toward it as the submachinegun fire started again.

Both Scoremasters were empty. Rourke tucked back, ramming the empty .45s into his belt, putting a fresh magazine up the well of the M-16, charging the chamber. "Rausch! We've got you! If you give it up, you'll be given a fair trial!"

There was laughter.

As John Rourke started to speak again, he felt the floor and walls tremble as a low roar consumed his hearing. A segment of the wall nearest him collapsed and he fell forward, covering his head with his hands and arms. Dust and falling debris were everywhere as he looked up.

"Rausch!"

Aldridge's voice came over Rourke's walkie-talkie. "He blew out the damn wall! You okay, Doctor?"

Rourke coughed, spat dust onto the floor, breathed into the walkie-talkie as he bent over it, trying to stand. "Yeah. All right. Get him!"

Rourke staggered toward the doorway into the corridor, pieces of the ceilings and walls everywhere, the corridor itself partially collapsed.

As Rourke edged forward, he could see the wall at the bend of the corridor. There was a hole in it large enough to have driven through with the pickup truck he stored at the Retreat. Freidrich Rausch was gone. On the floor, gleaming in the rubble, were dozens of empty brass cartridge cases. Rourke bent over, picking up several of these for possible later analysis. Each type of firearm from the period before The Night of The War had a distinctive firing pin indentation, as discernible to the careful observer armed with examples of firing pin indentations as the fingerprint, and just as unique. Rourke had such a work at the Retreat. If time allowed and circumstances dictated the research as beneficial, he could match the indentation on the physical samples he now pocketed to the appropriate firearm type—UZI, Steyr, Heckler and Koch, etc.—and, if he encountered such a weapon again, likely determine whether or not this specimen was the exact gun from which the case was ejected, providing of course that the firing pin hadn't been changed. Other markings as the case was ejected could be of use as well.

Visible through the hole were Aldridge and a half dozen men, a mixed force of U.S. Marines and German Commandoes, running into the snowy night.

Jason Darkwood leaned heavily against the corridor wall, holding his pistol in his right fist, his left arm limp at his side.

"What happened to you?" Rourke asked, approaching him. "Your left hand?"

"I figured if adrenaline screwed me up, more of it might burn the medication out of my system completely. Dropped a leg of the bed on my hand, Doctor. But it worked." The medical rationale was a bit dicey, but the principle seemed to have been sound enough in application, Rourke observed. "My head's killing me, my neck feels like somebody's standing on it, but I'm not shaking, my stomach isn't doing flip-flops and I'm in control again."

Rourke nodded, looking out into the snow, then turning his attention to Darkwood's hand. As gently as he could, Rourke began to examine it. Three fingers were broken, one in two places.

Aldridge and his men wouldn't get Rausch.

As he continued examining Darkwood's battered hand, John Rourke almost whispered, "God help us, now."

Chapter Sixteen

He made himself speak English. "How is the child who was with me? I must know!"

The German in the white laboratory coat with the stethoscope hanging at his throat smiled and, in English worse than Vassily Prokopiev's own, answered, "She is in good health, all things considered. In good health. With care, she will be well. Where did you find this child?"

"I must talk with Doctor John Rourke."

"Where have you heard of the Herr Doctor, young man?"

"I have a message for Doctor John Rourke."

"You have not asked about your own health."

"That does not matter."

"I will speak to my commanding officer. Perhaps you could tell him the message," the man smiled.

Prokopiev shook his head and his head hurt and he felt slightly sick. "I must speak with Doctor John Rourke. It is very important that I speak with Doctor John Rourke. I can speak with no one else. You must contact him."

"The Herr Doctor is a very busy man, young fellow."

"I am Vassily Prokopiev, Major of Elite Corps, Committee for State Security of the Soviet. I have important documents for Doctor Rourke. Only for Doctor Rourke."

"You were searched, young man, and there were no documents found on your person. You have had a serious time of it. Perhaps things will be clearer for you when you have rested. We will talk again, then."

Prokopiev tried sitting up as the doctor introduced the hypodermic needle to his arm.

"Doctor Rourke! I must see Doctor Rourke. It is very important that I give my message to Doctor—"

75

Chapter Seventeen

Michael Rourke, Paul Rubenstein and John Rourke entered Jason Darkwood's hospital room, Doctor Munchen already there, as were Sam Aldridge and Colonel Wolfgang Mann.

Sarah Rourke watched her son and her husband intently. Except for the touches of gray in John's hair and the subtle differences in attire and weapons, he and Michael could have been twin brothers rather than father and son. Their personalities were nearly as identical.

John took instant command of the meeting he had called, out of deference to Darkwood, here at the hospital. "I'll come right to the point, Sarah, gentlemen. Freidrich Rausch. I badly underestimated him, not badly enough that Commander Darkwood got killed but badly enough that personnel from both Mid-Wake and your command, Colonel, were killed. This man is very good. And, at least this time, he proved too good for me. He's on the loose, being helped by Dodd, most certainly, and part of Rausch's agenda doubtlessly includes finding you, Sarah, and killing you. That's a given. You should be safe at the Retreat," John said, smiling at her . . .

It was bitterly cold, and the partially finished walls of the Eden Base permanent structure complex provided little break against the wind and the snow driven on it.

Freidrich Rausch cupped his hands around a lighter and lit a cigarette. If Damien had a message for him, he knew where he would find it and he set to work. "Hold the light closer, Commander Dodd."

Freidrich Rausch took the skinny bladed commando knife and made an incision along his brother's abdomen, then began to lay back layers of skin and muscle, the cigarette still hanging from the right corner of his mouth, his eyes squinted against its smoke.

"God, I can't watch this."

"Then close your eyes, Dodd."

He cut through grayed and frozen tissue, at times sawing. At last he exposed the colon. He cut through it. His fingers stiff and numb in the rubber gloves, his brother radiating cold, he began searching, cutting, searching until, at last, he found a tiny synthetic capsule.

With the butt of his knife, he cracked the frozen surface of the water filled dish on top of his brother's chest, dropping the capsule into the water.

He spit out the cigarette butt onto the floor. "I knew he would not die without leaving me the means by which to continue our work," Freidrich Rausch said, a true feeling of pride filling him for his brother's devotion and foresight . . .

"I am at a loss, Doctor Rourke," Wolfgang Mann interjected. "I would feel more comfortable were I able to post troops surrounding the Retreat to protect the women inside; but, obviously, setting guards in the area would serve to alert any persons looking for Frau Rourke and the other women that they were present."

"One of us could stay with them," Michael said suddenly.

Sarah Rourke stood up. "We will be fine." She emphasized each word as she spoke. "Nobody can get inside the Retreat without using explosives or a laser or something, right? So, we'll be fine. A big pajama party." She tried using language she felt the men would understand. And, when John looked at her, she knew he understood very well.

Chapter Eighteen

Lieutenant Horst Hammerschmidt swung up into the saddle, his sergeant, Casmir Schlabrendorff giving the orders for the patrol to mount.

It was the kind of beautiful mountain morning which made it very difficult to remember there was a war going on and that enemy forces—those of the Soviet—lingered in the mountain passes and high valleys and in the jungles below, harassing New Germany's efforts to support the continuing struggles in Europe, Asia and American Georgia.

Periodically, he would remind his men of their commitment, as he had this morning after breakfast, before the tents were put down. "The Long Range Mountain Commando Group's mission is to ferret out the small units of Elite Corps personnel, thereby safeguarding the Air Corps of New Germany from surface to air missile attack, allowing the German people to prosecute the war against the Soviet Union and to assist their allies. You all know our mission. And I would never say that one of you ever forgets it. This unit has one of the best effectiveness ratings of any unit operating within the Long Range Mountain Commando Group. But still, Soviet surface to air missiles bring down or disable an average of three aircraft every five days. I would never say you do not try hard enough. But we must all try harder."

He kept his lectures to a minimum and as short as possible, most of his men little better than grown boys when he'd taken over the unit, used to long, boring parental lectures alternated with long and boring lectures from professors and military instructors. The last thing they needed was another father or teacher.

His older brother, Otto, had instilled early in him the idea that men—especially the highly trained volunteers who had earned the right to be called "Commandoes"—followed the example set for them by their leader, more so than any words. He had adopted that philosophy of leadership as well, never ordering his men to do something he would not do himself or had not already done.

The philosophy worked.

Some of the older military officers, men the age of Colonel Wolfgang Mann and above, but with less wisdom than the brilliant Mann, had theorized that, with the dissolution of the old order and the introduction of true republican democracy to New Germany, there would be a breakdown in military discipline. The opposite had proven to be the case.

The men fought, now, not for the leader, but for New Germany. And New Germany was their home for all the generations since the war between the two American and Soviet superpowers five centuries ago. Their wives, their sweethearts, mothers and sisters, all these lives were theirs to protect or squander and no man Horst Hammerschmidt had known showed any desire to shirk such responsibility.

His horse trembled beneath him and Hammerschmidt let the animal out into a canter for a few yards, wheeling, clapping him on the neck, whispering reassuringly to it. "Easy, Rommel, easy lad." The horse's head shook, as though he understood, and Horst Hammerschmidt would have wagered any man that Rommel did.

Sunlight streaked through a notch in the granite fortress walls of the mountains, the notch forming a pass in the higher altitudes toward which they would ride this morning, and the sunlight bathed Rommel's pale gray coat yellow.

Horst Hammerschmidt rose in his stirrups.

Sergeant Schlabrendorff called out, "The men are mounted and ready, Herr Lieutenant!"

Schlabrendorff saluted, holding it as Horst Hammerschmidt glanced along the column of twos. He returned the salute. "Order the men to move out in column of twos."

"Yes, Herr Lieutenant." Hammerschmidt lowered the salute.

Schlabrendorff did likewise, ordering over his shoulder, "In column of twos, forward!"

The Long Range Mountain Commandoes, their woodland camouflage uniforms as crisp as to be expected after already spending nine days in the field, their assault rifles slung across their backs, their saddles creaking, their horses looking as if somehow they were in a great hurry this morning and did not wish to be bothered moving at such a slow pace, passed him nearly to the last rank. Then Horst Hammerschmidt gently kneed Rommel, a slight tug to the left rein and his animal fell in to the column's left flank moving ahead easily, steam rising from his nostrils, already Hammerschmidt feeling the warmth of the animal's back through the split in the saddle's tree.

Leather boots and leather stirrups dully gleamed, the hoar frost's gray almost white against the near black of Rommel's stockinged forelegs.

Rommel shook his head, settling into the pace of Sergeant Schlabrendorff's big bay mare. "A beautiful morning, Schlabrendorff."

"Yes, Herr Lieutenant, very beautiful. But very cold for my old bones, I think."

Horst Hammerschmidt laughed and clapped Schlabrendorff on the back.

There was something in the air today. The animals felt it. So did he. For some reason, he touched at the flap of his belt holster, for the reassurance of his pistol there.

Chapter Nineteen

John Rourke stared through the window of the J7-V, a swirling blizzard of snow beneath its vertical take-off jets, the blizzard only slightly more intense than the storm surrounding Eden Base.

He watched Sarah.

Beside her stood Colonel Wolfgang Mann, and at some distance behind them, almost obscured by the snow, was a German gunship, the gunship's main rotor blades moving almost lazily.

Sarah was swathed in a German Arctic parka, but she pushed the hood back from her face, her hair catching in the wind, raising her hand to wave to him.

Although he knew she wouldn't be able to see him return the gesture, John Rourke returned it anyway. Mann would not leave her side, Rourke knew, until she and their daughter Annie and Natalia and Maria Leuden, Michael's mistress, were all safely ensconced together in the Retreat. There, at least, they could not be touched by the murderous Nazi Freidrich Rausch who wanted vengeance on Sarah because she had killed his brother while his brother, in turn, had been about to murder Akiro Kurinami.

And that would buy him the time he needed to find Rausch and destroy him. John Rourke could no longer see Sarah for the tempest of snow, but when he closed his eyes he could see her quite clearly again, her hand raised so gently to wave good-bye . . .

A microscope from the Eden Project stores handily solved the problem of reading the markings on the fragment of paper secured within the acid-proof capsule he'd removed from his dead brother's colon.

Perhaps Damien had utilized a magnifying instrument of some sort to see to make the markings. Commander Dodd could offer no clue and Freidrich Rausch could only guess, never know.

But on the piece of paper was drawn a map. The markings were very basic, but clearly designed to match with topographic figures from a larger map.

At the rough center of the most prominent feature—a mountain—there was drawn a star. At the center of the star a solitary letter was written: the letter "R."

Chapter Twenty

The outer door of the Retreat closed and, her mother beside her, Annie Rubenstein crossed through the red lit area between outer and inner doors, then began closing the inner door as well. The shawl she had cocooned about her shoulders against the icy blast of the outside world began to slip to her forearms, her mother saying, "Let me get that," and stepping past her to finish securing the door.

Annie let the shawl fall completely away, then, neatly folding it, holding it against her while her mother completed the task of sealing them inside the Retreat.

Her mother, wearing blue slacks and pink maternity style top Annie had made for her, stepped away from the door. "So. Now we're all locked up and ready for the pajama party, aren't we?" Her mother's lips smiled, but Sarah Rourke's voice did not. "You're the only one who really has nothing to settle, here. You're happy."

Annie started to say something, not quite sure what her mother wanted her to say, when she heard Maria Leuden's voice from the kitchen. "I have the cocoa made, Frau Rourke."

"Sarah. Call me Sarah, Maria," Annie's mother said, walking past Annie, down the three steps into the Great Room and starting across it.

Annie followed her mother with her eyes, started again to speak but all motion—her own, her mother's, Maria's behind the kitchen counter—suddenly stopped when the door from one of the spare bedrooms opened. Natalia Anastasia Tiemerovna stood there, her almost black hair darker-looking somehow, longer-looking too, than Annie had remembered it being. It was illusion, only, a trick of perception, but the illusion was truly beautiful. Natalia wore her hair past her shoulders and as she moved from the doorway, her hair moved, as if, almost, it had life of its own. A simple maroon blouse, open at the throat, full sleeves that ended in long cuffs tight at her

83

wrists, the blouse of something that looked like silk, a pale rose colored skirt, very full and so long it came to her ankles, she was a marriage of elegance and simplicity.

Natalia walked down the three steps into the Great Room.

Her slender, high waist made her legs look impossibly long.

Her hair flowed in rhythm with her clothing.

Her cheekbones — so high — accentuated the deep pansy blueness of her eyes.

Natalia's left hand slipped into the slit pocket at the side seam of her skirt, her right hand extended as though touching gently at the invisible hand of a man who should have been there but wasn't.

The effect was very much like that of someone of incredible beauty on her way to a palace ball.

She was perfect.

But Natalia was always perfect, had been before her nervous breakdown and was again.

The permanence of Natalia's being — her looks, her capableness, everything about her — was something in which Annie had always taken considerable comfort. She didn't know why, really, but she had. That, almost equally balanced with the genuine friendship Annie felt for Natalia, had determined that she risk her own sanity in helping Natalia to regain hers.

Natalia stopped at the base of the steps, the toe of her left foot on the bottom step behind her. "I understand we have come here for two reasons. For our safety against the Nazi murderer Rausch and to sort some things out in our personal lives. That seems obvious, doesn't it? I think I am more or less recovered and the doctors at Mid-Wake tell me that as well. Perhaps a good glass of whiskey after the cocoa might be best, hmm?"

Natalia crossed the Great Room, toward the counter where Maria Leuden stood holding a cup in one hand and a saucepan in the other, as if she were a child playing statue. Natalia swept her skirt under her as she perched atop one of the stools beside the counter.

Annie crossed the Great Room, setting down the gray crocheted shawl on the arm of the sofa, as if staking a claim to that spot for later. She approached the counter and took another of the stools, at the end of the counter, sat, arranged her clothes, waited. Natalia placed cigarettes and a lighter taken from a pocket on the counter. Like her father's, the lighter was a Zippo, but slimmer and almost new-looking.

Her mother went around the counter, took a large glass ashtray from inside one of the cabinets and set it on the counter near Natalia. Maria poured the cocoa. It smelled rich, good. The Germans grew cocoa beans in Argentina and the cocoa was very fresh. Her mother sat down on Maria's side of the counter, knitting her fingers into a fragile looking tent, staring down at her hands. "I don't know how long we'll be here, maybe a few days, maybe a few weeks. So I think we ought to talk about several things. With John and Michael and Paul away, this may be the only chance the four of us will have to thrash things out."

Sarah Rourke moved her hands, pressed her left hand over Annie's hands which were on her lap. "My daughter here is the only one of us who's happy, I think." And she looked at Annie searchingly. "Aren't you?"

Annie shrugged her shoulders, her hands still in her lap, her mother's hand still over them. "I don't know if happy is the right word." Cocoa steamed in all four cups now, Maria taking the saucepan to the sink, running water into the pan to rinse it for easier cleaning later. "I'm very happy being Paul's wife, if that's what you mean. I wish we could have a baby, but we both think we should wait until this is all over. That's just our idea, though. I'm happy Natalia's well and back with us again."

She exchanged smiles with Natalia as Natalia lit a cigarette. Natalia exhaled a long, thin stream of smoke through her lips. "I would never have recovered were it not for you, Annie." Natalia cast her eyes down, picked a speck of lint from her skirt.

"So, I'm happy about a lot of things," Annie went on, "but, like all of us, I guess, there's a lot bothering me. The obvious things though. I'm frustrated that this war with the Soviets keeps going on and on and getting bigger all the time. And I'm afraid for Paul and for Michael and for Daddy, especially, because, well, he's always in the middle of it all and he and Paul especially—when Michael and I were just children—they were risking their lives every day and they still do."

"You are worrying, I think, about the odds, aren't you, Annie?" Maria Leuden almost whispered.

Sarah Rourke blew gently on the cocoa in her cup, moving her hand, placing both hands around the cup as she sipped from it.

"I'm worried about the odds," Annie nodded. "I have three of them to lose. I mean, we all do in a way. Without Paul, I'd be dead inside."

She could hear Natalia exhale.

She didn't look at her mother, shifted her position a little bit on the stool, unnecessarily smoothed the gray woolen full skirt she wore.

Her mother spoke. "When you talk about being dead inside, Ann, I think you're addressing the problem here. There are three men and four women. Two of the women have a very serious problem that has no solution. One of the women has a problem she may not even be aware of."

"Didn't they used to call these sorts of talks 'bitch sessions'?" Natalia asked, flicking ashes from her cigarette.

Sarah Rourke smiled. "I think they did. You and I know our problem. We've had it, still have it, will have it. So let's talk about Maria and Michael for a minute."

"That is not—"

Sarah Rourke looked intently at Maria Leuden, Annie watching her face in profile.

Maria was very pretty, her auburn hair pulled back, caught up at the nape of her neck with a print scarf tied into a floppy bow, her eyes guarded behind the lenses of her wire-rimmed glasses.

Annie's mother said, "Michael is exactly like his father, all of the virtues and all of the faults. Do you know what John Rourke's fatal flaw is?"

Annie didn't like the word fatal.

"Any of you?" Sarah Rourke insisted.

Natalia stubbed out her cigarette, looking into the ashtray as she spoke. "He is perfect, isn't that it?"

"Five points for the lady from the Soviet Union," Sarah Rourke laughed, the laughter hollow-sounding, sending a chill up along Annie's spine. She hugged her arms over her breasts. "John Rourke is so perfect it's hard to remember he's human. I realized that. But I was like Maria is with Michael. It was like being touched by a god or something, being favored by someone from Mt. Olympus. 'You have been honored as has no other woman.' Like that. So, I know." Sarah Rourke looked at Maria Leuden. Annie unfolded her arms and clutched her cup of cocoa, sipping at it. It warmed her, but not enough. "Tell me how you feel, if you can, Maria. I mean, don't you feel the same way with Michael? Like there's something so much better about him simply because he is who he is, that it's a privilege to wash his socks?"

Maria Leuden actually blushed.

"What are you trying to say?" Natalia asked very softly, setting down her cocoa. "And we would have been better off with the whiskey, I think."

"I'm not trying to hurt anyone," Annie's mother said. "All I'm trying to do is get to the core of a problem three of us have, but really four of us are affected by. Who appointed John the protector of the world? And Paul and Michael his deputies? Who?"

"They're men," Annie said, not consciously thinking about speaking, just blurting it out. "They didn't have to be appointed by anyone."

Sarah Rourke laughed, sipped her cocoa. "You watched too many westerns out of the tape library, Annie. Don't you mean, 'A man's gotta do what a man's gotta do'?"

Annie wished she smoked. It would give her something to do with her hands besides folding them in her lap. As she looked down at her hands, she realized she was pinching the fabric of her skirt. She shook her head. "I don't mean that, but maybe it sounds like that. But the three of them are—"

"What? If you follow your reasoning, think about it. Shouldn't Paul almost be pictured as a dove carrying an olive branch and—"

"Momma! What—I know how you feel, but—" Annie started.

"No, you don't know how I feel," Sarah Rourke whispered, clearing her throat. "I love your father. Natalia loves your father. Neither one of us has a prayer. And Maria's setting herself up for the same thing, the same heartbreaks. You fell in love with a man and you're happy. None of us did. I guess that's what I'm saying. Paul rises above himself. He always has, hasn't he? I mean, even in the aftermath of that plane crash they both survived on The Night of The War. Who was the one who had the courage to stick with John regardless of his safety, simply because he knew it was the decent thing to do? That's a man. For your father, Annie, there wasn't any question. His nature just demanded it. 'The pilot and the co-pilot are dying or dead? Hey, poor guys. Don't worry, everyone, I can fly the plane. You say we're outnumbered by renegade bikers? No big deal! Remember, I'm here and I'm John Thomas Rourke, doctor of medicine, survival expert, weapons expert, CIA trained, rah rah! So, don't be afraid'."

"No!" Annie said. She stood up. She didn't know what she wanted to say or if she wanted to just stand there, sit back down, or go to the bedroom she would share with Natalia.

Before she could make up her mind, Maria Leuden stood, began to speak. "I think we need lunch now." She walked toward the little cupboard on the far wall, opened it, took out a bib fronted apron and tied it over her dress. "I love Michael and I realize he is special, very special. But then, I wouldn't love him if he were not, would I?" She took some of the fresh eggs Wolfgang Mann had gotten for them — flown in from New Germany — and started placing them on the counter. "Is an omelette all right? I love cooking omelettes."

"Yes," Natalia said. "But only if you let me help." She stood up quickly, went to the cupboard, found an apron, began putting it on. Annie just watched.

Maria Leuden was talking again, her voice sounding odd. "I don't know if he wants to marry me or if he still loves his dead wife too much or—" Maria Leuden dropped an egg onto the floor, then dropped to her knees, bringing the apron up in front of her face, weeping loudly.

Annie's hands were trembling.

Natalia went to her knees beside Maria, folding the girl into her arms.

Annie Rourke Rubenstein looked at her mother.

Sarah Rourke stood up, went to the counter, took one of the rinseable German fabric towels — like reusable paper towels — and began to mop up the egg.

Annie wanted to cry, too.

She cleared her throat. "Omelettes are fine for little old ladies. Not us. How about steaks? Natalia? Give me a hand. Get out some of those fresh onions. I mean, we won't be kissing anybody so we don't have to worry about eating onions, right? Maria? Maria!"

Maria Leuden — she looked as if she felt hopeless — stared at Annie. She was still on her knees beside where the egg had fallen and cracked.

"Maria — you come back to the freezer with me. I'll need your help. Momma?"

Sarah Rourke looked at her, smiling a little. "You pour us all a

88

drink. Make mine some of the Seagrams, please. The stuff Daddy had them make for us."

Sarah Rourke nodded.

"Mine, too," Natalia added. "Bring back some of the dehydrated potatoes, Annie."

Annie looked at Maria. Maria was standing up now, arms limp at her sides, tears running down her cheeks. Then Annie looked at her mother. "The same for Maria." And then Annie took the girl by her elbow and started propelling her out of the kitchen, toward the storage room where the large freezers were. "Germans make terrific desserts, I understand. Will you show me how to make something really special, Maria?" The girl didn't say a word, only sniffed, daubing with the hem of her apron at the corners of the tear-glistening hazel eyes shielded by her glasses.

Chapter Twenty-one

His dapple gray horse, Rommel, was the finest steed he had ever ridden and he had taken every opportunity he could since his boyhood to ride. He had named Rommel after the almost universally respected German Field Marshal of World War Two. And now, Rommel was shifting nervously, tossing his black mane, snorting his flared nostrils at the wind. Such behavior was frequently a sign of something about to happen. Horst Hammerschmidt saw no rhyme or reason for the animal's having some sixth sense of possible danger, but Rommel seemed to and Hammerschmidt heeded the warning.

"Sergeant."

"Yes, Herr Lieutenant?"

"Extend the column anticipating possible attack. Then deploy two outriders to standard distance front and rear of the column. Have everyone check their weapons."

"Yes, Herr Lieutenant."

Horst Hammerschmidt listened only half-heartedly as Schlabrendorff echoed and amplified on the orders given him. He could also hear the rattle of slings, the movement of bolts. He patted the pistol holstered at his right side. But these ambient sounds—like the wind, the crackling of dislodging gravel pieces beneath the horses' hooves as they trailed upward along the gradually rising granite apron—he forced from his consciousness.

He listened for something else. The drawing of a bolt, the scrape of metal or synthetic against rock or fabric, the cracking of a pine twig in the rocks above them.

And his eyes were squinted against the gray clouds and gray rocks, watching intently each patch of green for something moving in black, the uniform color of the KGB Elite Corps.

"All is in order, Herr Lieutenant!" Schlabrendorff announced.

Horst Hammerschmidt nodded, almost whispering the words,

"Very good, Schlabrendorff. Be ready." And Hammerschmidt stroked Rommel's wide forehead as he leaned forward in the saddle.

The crack of a rifle shot, but he felt the pain across his shoulder blades before he heard the shot. Hammerschmidt lurched over his animal's neck, his right fist knotting in Rommel's mane, his left hand clutching at the horse's bridle.

Rommel vaulted ahead.

Hammerschmidt began to shout, but there was a sound over the crack of rifle shots from the rocks above, a sound like nothing he had ever heard before. "Casmir! Deploy the men!"

Hammerschmidt drew back on Rommel's mane, his feet slipping from the stirrups, finding them again, numbness creeping ahead of the pain which spread across his back and shoulders and neck in a wave, a green wash over his eyes. He lowered his head, knotting both fists into Rommel's mane now.

The animal reared.

The sound.

Rommel's eyes were fear-wide and red-rimmed.

The sound, like the buzzing of some huge insect. A crater appeared in the granite before them, a puff of smoke and dust forming into a mushroom shaped cloud, Rommel rearing again, then leaping through the cloud and over the crater.

The buzzing.

Another explosion.

Another explosion.

Another.

More bursts of automatic weapons fire.

"They are all dead!"

Schlabrendorff?

"Corporal! Look out!"

Another explosion.

More gunfire.

The green wash was a blanket covering him, chilling his stomach, making his head light, nausea rising from the pit of his stomach.

Three black uniforms. A peculiar looking gun in the hands of one of the Elite corpsmen, like a full-sized heavy machine gun, but so odd looking.

Its barrel seemed to pulse with light.

The rocks near Rommel exploded, the horse bolting forward,

91

straight toward the men. Rommel was climbing from the granite trail into the rocks, slipping, catching his footing, scrambling upward, running on. Schlabrendorff's bay stumbled, pitching Schlabrendorff to the rocks. One of the Elite Corpsmen, his face and even his uniform covered in the green wash flooding over Horst Hammerschmidt's eyes, swung an assault rifle toward Schlabrendorff. As he started to fire, Horst Hammerschmidt drew back on Rommel's mane with all his strength, Rommel skidding on his haunches along a slick outcropping of granite, shale spraying up in the animal's wake as Hammerschmidt wrenched his body upright, his right hand releasing Rommel's mane. His pistol. His fist closed over it, somehow the flap open. He drew the pistol and pointed it toward the green apparition of the Elite Corpsman and fired it out into the man's head and thorax.

Rommel reared.

Hammerschmidt could hold on no longer. The green wash flooded over him completely, suddenly green no longer, only black and cold.

Chapter Twenty-two

It was too early in the day for serious drinking and Natalia merely sipped at her second glass of whiskey.

Whiskey was wonderfully like a man. The first time it entered, it was warm, so hot it was like fire. Afterward, as it entered again and again, there was the mellowness of possession and being possessed.

She turned her thoughts away from that. There was only one man who possessed her, ever would. And he treated her as though he did not possess her at all because he could not treat her otherwise. His sense of honor, of course.

Annie sat in the farthest corner of the sofa, her legs tucked up under a voluminous dark gray woolen skirt, her shawl wrapped tightly around her, her eyes not smiling. The beautifully tied bow which formed the collar of the white blouse Annie wore seemed to droop nearly as much as the corners of Annie's tightly drawn lips.

Maria sat in the reclining chair, but the chair was not reclined, almost as bolt upright as Maria's posture within it, hands tightly clasped to one another in her lap, knees close together beneath a black uniform skirt. Natalia knew the look. Hold yourself very tightly because otherwise you will burst. She knew the look because she had burst.

Sarah drank the funny tasting cola John had the Germans make for him. It was almost the correct formula, but not quite. German scientists had worked quite diligently, she was given to understand, to analyze the soft drink from five centuries ago which John had preserved here. Almost successful.

She couldn't stand to drink it, wondered if she would have killed for a bottle of the original, told herself she would not. More than the taste, it was the nostalgia of having it. But some things, no matter how good they felt or what memories they rekindled, weren't worth death.

Her nervous breakdown was the best thing that had ever happened to her, Natalia realized now. It had taken her off the treadmill of survival and combat, given her the chance for introspection, self-analysis. Her situation in life was hopeless, but there was life itself. And she enjoyed the sensation of life now more than she had since years before the Night of the War.

Maria began to talk, as though confessing under truth drugs. "I met Michael when we were about to leave for Egypt to try to stop the Soviets from using their horrible gas." The gas, a pet project of Natalia's late husband, Vladmir Karamatsov, reacted with male hormones, virtually transforming men into homicidal beasts. "It's not easy being a woman and being academically smart. I was always smart. The girls resent that, and the boys resent it even more. You try to hide being smart, but you have to be clever. I never learned where they drew the line between the two, being smart and being clever. But Michael liked me. For what I am." Maria stopped speaking, as though catching her breath between phrases in a catechism she'd memorized only half-well and was afraid to forget if she lost its rhythm. "He loves me," she added, as though she had, indeed, forgotten the rest.

Natalia, lighting a cigarette, smiled at her. "You are very beautiful, Maria. And, so is Michael, for that matter. You and I have a great deal in common. The Rourke man you adore is still in love with a dead wife, you think. The one I adore is in love with his living one, I know." Natalia made the light, exhaled smoke quickly, picked up her glass of whiskey and raised the glass toward Sarah in a mock toast.

Sarah laughed.

Natalia sipped.

Annie looked uncomfortable, shifted uneasily, rearranged her shawl.

Maria spoke again. "Sarah is right. He is like some sort of god from mythology. Powerful and strong and beautiful. When he makes love to me—" She stopped speaking suddenly, looked at Sarah, blushed and looked away.

Annie almost whispered, "This is really tacky. Realize what we sound like?"

Annie's mother said, "You sound like a Rourke. I'm only that by marriage. It would stand to reason—and I love you very much and couldn't ask for a finer daughter—but it only makes sense that if a male Rourke is a perfect man, then a female Rourke should be a perfect woman? I mean, right? Think about yourself, okay? You're a better cook than I ever was. You design and sew well enough, you could have been the top name in Paris five centuries ago. Your hair is so beautiful—there were women who would have killed for hair as pretty as yours, you know that? You eat like a man, you always have. And you don't put on a pound? Hasn't it ever dawned on you that you're as perfect as they are? You always dress like Annie Oakley on her way to the senior prom. I mean, I'm not criticizing you. I'm just saying, you can fight better than almost any man, you're a crack shot, you can do everything. Hasn't that hit you? You're the perfect woman. Intuitive—you can even read people's minds."

"I never got to go to a prom," Annie said to her lap, not looking at her mother. Her voice barely above a whisper, Annie added, "And I am not perfect."

"But you are," Sarah said. "Michael asserted his perfection earlier. But as a girl, it was more perfect for you to keep your perfection low key. And you didn't even have to think about it. It was just the way to be. What can't you do, Annie?"

"Shall we concede that exceptional parents make exceptional children, Sarah?" Natalia remarked, exhaling cigarette smoke, trying to turn the conversation from Annie who looked like she'd had enough the moment the conversation began before dinner and, despite her mother's remarks to the contrary, had barely eaten a thing.

"I wasn't exceptional, Natalia," Sarah said.

Natalia studied the tip of her cigarette, kicked out of her shoes and drew her legs up under the hem of her skirt.

"Your real father, I understand, was a firebrand, a genius," Sarah went on. "Your mother was a ballerina with the Bolshoi," Sarah said slowly. "A superior mind and a superior body. What are you but the result of your genes?"

Natalia flicked ashes into the ashtray. "That almost sounds like fascism, Sarah," Natalia smiled. "But what are Michael and Annie, but half the result—each of them—of your genes? Hmm? I'm not perfect. John's perfect, but only because he doesn't realize that he is, would never presume to even think that he is. That's his true perfection. And Michael's and Annie's, too.

"Annie's genius for design. Think about that," Natalia pressed. "You're so average, Sarah? Hmm? How many women begin a career as an artist after studying to be a nurse and never studying art at all and then become both artist and writer, critically acclaimed for both? All the while raising a family and coping with a collapsing marriage—" That would have hurt and Natalia didn't want it to but it had to be said.

"—and an absentee husband? How many women who had never camped out much if at all, never fired a gun, totally refused to prepare for any sort of violence at all, never had any military or survival training, could have done what you did on The Night of the War and afterward? You saved yourself, you protected your two young children, you managed to become quite the heroine. I've listened to a lot of stories your children have told me about you. Your trouble is that in your heart you feel you should still be the liberal you always were. You rose to the occasion out of your liberalism and you're almost embarrassed by it, guilty for it and you want all of this to end—just like the rest of us do—but you want to go back to your comfortable ideals. You can't ever go back, because you know what the real world is like. You see, I can say that because I was never a good Communist."

Sarah just looked at her, Sarah's fingers touching at her abdomen—the baby. Natalia exhaled smoke. "It took me a long time to realize that, but I never was. I was born into Communism, raised a Communist and because of that I never really considered the alternatives with any seriousness. All I thought was that I wanted to fight for the welfare of the people. And that hasn't changed. But I realized that what I was doing was having directly the opposite effect. It's like you with your liberalism. You believed in peace, you believed that violence was an evil. Violence is only an evil when it's practiced by the evil. When violence is used to counter evil, it is no longer an evil. It is only unfortunate."

"The end justifies the means, Natalia?" Sarah asked, not really asking at all, almost taunting, leaning forward, something in her eyes making Sarah look as if she were about to cry.

"Peace is still a worthy ideal, Sarah. It's why we're all fighting. But the very basis of hardcore liberal idealism in which you believed was what allowed evil to flourish and precipitated the very violence you abhorred. The end doesn't justify any means or every means. But depending on the circumstances—that's situational ethics, not Communism—some ends justify some means. We all do what we have to do. We are all who we have to be. Just like you have to be in love with John and I have to be in love with him, too. And Maria is in love with Michael. And Annie is good at everything she tries. And John is heroic and Michael is heroic and Paul is heroic. Nobody told Paul to be heroic. He did what he had to do. Not just because circumstances dictated that or because his very being dictated that, but for both reasons. Circumstance could have dictated anything, and if Paul hadn't been Paul,

96

he wouldn't have responded the way he had.

"I know we're all here to thrash things out," Natalia concluded. "But we can't predicate that on blaming ourselves for who we are or what we are. We have to work within the framework of our identities, not cry over who we are." She shouldn't have used that word — "cry" — Natalia realized almost as she said it, Sarah's tears coming, Natalia slipping off the couch and dropping to her knees beside Sarah, hugging her to her . . .

Freidrich Rausch sat in the tunnel of foundation materials beneath one of the partially completed modules of Eden Base. The wind howled beyond the confines of his meager shelter as he stroked one of the stiletto-bladed knife's edges over the stone, the yellow light of the lamp his only companion. Taped onto the cold radiating wall, the tape at one corner dropping down from moisture which condensed and almost instantly froze from his breathing, was a map.

The mountains of Northeastern American Georgia.

He stared at one mountain's shape now.

Inside that mountain was not only Rourke's wife, but Rourke's daughter (the wife of Rourke's best friend, the man a Jew), the mistress of Rourke' s son and the mysterious Russian woman who was said to be Rourke's own mistress.

When he killed them all, not just Rourke's wife who had killed his — Rausch's — brother, the great Herr Doctor Rourke would be undone. So consumed with vengeance that his effectiveness would be destroyed, it would be possible to go ahead with plans both here, in Eden, and in New Germany.

He set down his knife, picked up the flask of liquor and removed the stopper. He took a strong swallow, a toast to Rourke's mountain and the promise it held.

And the women there, who would not have to die exactly immediately.

Chapter Twenty-three

Snow was drifted all about them, a shimmering wall of white the consistency of the frosting on a cake, swirled by the wind. The hurricane which was now blown out in the Gulf of Mexico, this was its legacy.

To be forced down in such a storm was not unique, but to be forced down such a short distance from one's own base and to be trapped by the near zero visibility was intolerable because there was so much to do. The storm would have all but halted the restoration of fortifications surrounding Eden Base. The only consolation was that the Soviet forces would be equally handicapped, slowed down, he hoped.

Wolfgang Mann spent the time reviewing orders, studying maps and computer projections—preoccupied.

He had taken his turn working to repair the fuel line, been the last of his shift to return to the comparative warmth of the gunship, the pilot and three of the commando unit comprising the alternating shift. Mann had ordered that no person be exposed to the numbing cold for more than fifteen minutes at a time, their arctic gear not suited to the blizzard conditions surrounding them.

With any luck, this last shift would have the fuel line repaired and it would be possible to start the main rotor again, the batteries kept warm and ready. It would require time in order to properly warm the engine powering the main rotor to the point where the machine could be flown out. Synth-oil turned to something nearer the consistency of glue under these conditions. Scientists at New Germany worked to develop better suited lubricants but this was here, this was now. If the winds would ever decrease to the point where take-off would be possible, and the machine were warmed by then, perhaps—

Wolfgang Mann threw down his pencil in disgust. In an age where so much was computerized, he had always thought better with a pencil and blank paper, preferred to make real marks on real maps and, only then, transfer to computer.

And he was preoccupied, could not properly concentrate anyway, had welcomed his tour at repairing the fuel line—he could not take his mind from Sarah Rourke and he was ashamed of his thoughts. Sarah Rourke was the wife of another man, bore that man's child in her body, and that man was fine and good and more noble than any man he had ever known. And his own wife—there had not even been the occasion to fly back to New Germany for her funeral service—was only recently taken from him.

He had loved his wife and she loved him, but they had never been friends, really. His work, her volunteerism, all of that and many other factors, many beautiful things in common, the basis of fond memories which filled him with sadness more deep than he had ever felt, at the mere thought of her passing. But they had never been friends.

The fault for that was almost entirely his own, Wolfgang Mann realized. He had never thought of friendship with a woman, hence never attempted it, nor thought of friendship breeding feelings he dared not even speak.

Women were different from men. He smiled at the brilliance of his insight. But they were, or so he had always thought. They had things which interested them which no man was interested in and they, in turn, could not be bothered with the things of men. But he had oriented his thinking always toward the external, never to personal qualities, thoughts, observations, shared emotions beyond passion.

Sarah Rourke was extraordinary.

He smiled as he thought that she should have been German.

He could never tell her his thoughts. Aside from how embarrassed such thoughts would make her feel, she would likely cease to be his friend.

And, somehow, he would have a new sort of emptiness with which to deal, with which to live.

And he worried now. Four women, no matter the strength of the Herr Doctor's mountain Retreat, no matter the skills of Fraulein Major Tiemerovna, four women would be no match for Freidrich Rausch.

Wolfgang Mann looked back at his charts.

He snapped his pencil between his fingers, without really thinking of it.

He could send troops to guard the Retreat, despite the fact that

Doctor Rourke—and everyone, really—had felt it best not to draw attention to the specific location by placing personnel in the immediate area.

Wolfgang Mann told himself all the things that he could to reassure himself. They had primary and backup radio capability. Regardless of the weather, a good pilot could take-off and land a J7-V close enough to the Retreat, and with a few volunteers give this maniac Rausch what he deserved.

And the Retreat was a veritable arsenal of conventional weapons, was sealed within granite and steel, its entrance disguised so well that it would be impossible to discern, especially now, snow certainly drifted over any telltale markings by the entrance, over the rock counter-balances themselves.

She—they were safe.

There was a blast of bitterly cold wind and a wash of icy spicules of snow blew across the interior of the cabin.

"Herr Colonel! The fuel line! All is in order!"

Chapter Twenty-four

The radio message was encoded and it took almost a minute for the radio operator aboard the J7-V to decrypt. "Request landing at following coordinates. Emergency."

The pilot of the J7-V looked up at John Rourke. "What should I do, Herr General?"

John Rourke had totally dismissed his appointment to the rank of brigadier general by the president of Mid-Wake, and, fortunately, so had most of the persons with whom he regularly associated. The young German pilot was another story. "Does the message appear genuine, Lieutenant?"

The lieutenant looked at the radio operator. The radio operator said, "With your permission, Herr General. The message appears authentic. The decryption key is proper."

Rourke looked over the lower control panel set in the cockpit dash and toward the cloud layer beneath them. Nothing was visible to the naked eye but clouds, an endless and enormous gray sea of them. "What do your sensors show?" Rourke asked the copilot and navigator.

"There appear to be heavy concentrations of helicopter gunships—German, Herr General—both in the air and on the ground. There are no other vehicles in evidence."

"Anything else?"

"There are signs of human habitation, Herr General."

Michael spoke from behind him. "Dad, these coordinates match the coordinates for one of the villages the Wild Tribes people were relocated to, to protect them."

"I don't like this," Paul murmured, looking at the map beside Michael as Rourke looked back.

"Take us down, Lieutenant. Give it a flyby at a decent altitude that'll allow more detailed observation. If everything appears satisfactory, bring us in. That fellow who wants to see me can keep for a little while."

"Yes, Herr General!"

As Rourke walked aft, he heard Paul saying under his breath, "Herr General."

John Rourke looked at his friend and smiled. Rourke took his seat, seeing to the security of his weapons first because of the anticipated landing, the twin stainless Detonics Combat Masters still on his body in the double Alessi shoulder rig . . .

Paul Rubenstein sluffed into his arctic parka, shivering, the cold having nothing to do with it. As he stared out the rapidly steaming-over window, he could hardly believe his eyes. Modular buildings of the same construction employed by the Germans in their field hospitals and other field accommodations of a permanent or semi-permanent nature, sliced in half, as though ripped apart, but blackened at the center.

The battered old Browning High Power that had been nearly as constant a companion to him as John Rourke since the Night of the War—it was holstered now in the rig John had dug out for him from supplies kept at the Retreat. This was the first time he'd had the chance to use it. "This was made by DeSantis. They called it the 'Slant Shoulder Holster.' Thumb break instead of a trigger guard break, like my rig. I hadn't remembered I had it, but I was involved in a job with the FBI's Special Operations Group a couple of years before the Night of the War. They swore by the High Power, some of the guns having more than forty thousand rounds through them with just a change of barrel and a few minor parts. I needed the holster because I was told to use the same gun the FBI unit used, all the same equipment so I'd be indistinguishable from them." And then John Rourke had smiled, "But I had a .45 under my clothes." John Rourke and the .45 ACP were an inseparable combination, Paul Rubenstein realized. Yet John had never been so closed-minded as to say the .45 was the only gun to carry. John carried and used .357s and .44 Magnums and on at least one occasion Paul could remember had said, "More important than the caliber is the accuracy and skill with which it's employed, and that translates to the man behind the gun. For all practical purposes, a .45 ACP and a decently constructed 9mm hollow point have about the same effect on a target barring extenuating circumstances. That was a debate which raged for years after the Army adopted a 9mm pistol. A lot of the same people who were complaining were the same people who still used Hardball in their .45s, too. The stone age must have been a wonderful era because so many people were nostalgic for it."

The fuselage door opened and Paul Rubenstein, pulling up his hood and hiding his hands in his pockets, followed John Rourke out into the gray cold. No snow fell.

What weapon was this, which had wreaked such horrible destruction here? Not artillery; not explosives.

There was no sound, except for the beating of the rotor blades of German gunships overhead and the cooling of the J7-V's jet engines. The snow fell so evenly it was like a curtain, silent and cold.

The wind was totally still.

Bodies lay everywhere, many only charred lumps hardly recognizable as once human beings who fought to stay alive, loved, nurtured, some few of the bodies covered with blankets or inside black body bags, hundreds more of them exposed to the cold, but beyond caring.

"God bless them," Paul Rubenstein murmured, closing his eyes for an instant, turning his head away.

He heard Michael saying, "I've never seen any pattern of destruction like this. What—"

Paul opened his eyes and turned to look as John Rourke spoke. "It's an energy weapon. It has to be. Like nothing we have."

"The Soviets' Particle Beam weapons," Paul almost whispered.

John looked at him.

"What if they'd found a way to miniaturize and developed some sort of power source for them," Paul offered. "The technology seems impossible, but what if it isn't? What if the Soviets used this village as some sort of testing site to determine operational characteristics in the field?"

"I don't think we could counter an energy weapon with anything we have," Michael added, turning his head, looking away. "All those people—my God."

And John Rourke made the sign of the cross.

Paul Rubenstein had a different faith, but the same emotion. "Amen."

Chapter Twenty-five

It was late, but none of them at least admitted to feeling at all like sleeping and, after all, Sarah had called it a "pajama party" anyway.

Natalia was nearly dressed for it, down to her bra and a pair of Chinese silk tap pants. As she hung up the pale rose colored skirt she'd worn earlier, her eyes caught a glimpse of something else hanging in the back of the closet. Most of her things had been sent ahead of her and, tired after the long trip from Mid-Wake, she had wanted desperately to rest. Annie had asked if she—Natalia—would like her things unpacked and Natalia had agreed.

At the back of the closet hung one of the black jumpsuits Natalia wore almost like a combat uniform. She had several of them, of course, one or two stored here at the Retreat—at least two, come to think of it—and two more in the remaining two pieces of luggage not yet unpacked.

Did this one, the one hanging in the closet, belong to a different Natalia Anastasia Tiemerovna, she wondered, or did it still belong to her?

She finished hanging up her skirt and walked over to the smaller of the three suitcases, the open one. It was beside the bed and she dropped to her knees, moving aside her black bag, the one which doubled as large purse and small rucksack. Beneath the bag, exposed now, was her gunbelt, the two full-flap holsters bound together with it.

She unbound them, setting holsters and belt on the bed, still kneeling at the bed's edge. The black leather gleamed dully, recently saddle-soaped and oiled, the holsters and the matching revolvers they held nearly lost when the helicopter had crashed and Annie had kept both she and Otto Hammerschmidt alive in the water until Jason Darkwood's submarine had come for them.

Annie had cared for her guns and her holsters and her knife and the care showed, everything good as new despite the dousing.

Natalia took up the holsters and belt and, one at a time, opened the holsters' flaps, then withdrew the revolvers carried within.

They were Smith and Wesson Model 686s, four-inch barreled adjustable sighted L-Frame .357 Magnums, customized by a man John had known—Ron Mahovsky—and bearing on the right barrel flats (the barrels ground flat on both sides, lightening them slightly) American eagles, wings spread in challenge, eyes keen and alert. The guns had been given to her by the first and only president of U.S. II, the transitional government of the United States after the death of the president on the Night of the War and before the Great Conflagration, when the ionized atmosphere had caught fire and almost all life on earth was destroyed. His name had been Chambers.

He had told her he wanted to give her a medal, for her role in aiding in the evacuation of peninsula Florida before and during the great earthquake which had caused the peninsula to separate from the panhandle and fall into the sea. But he had told her also that he had no medal to give and, considering she was an officer with the forces of the foreign invader with which the United States was at war, he could not have given her one if he had.

So, instead, he had given her these pistols and the holsters for them, once a gift to him.

The belt that accompanied them had been horribly large for her woman's waist, but John had found a belt for her and—"John," Natalia whispered.

The revolvers in both her hands, she studied them for a moment. The things she had done with them, lives taken and lives saved.

Natalia replaced the Smith and Wessons in their holsters and set the guns and gunbelt back in the small suitcase. The revolvers were empty, but there was ammunition in the small suitcase as well.

She left them empty, stood, reached up her hands behind her back and removed her bra . . .

Annie had made a light snack for them while Natalia dressed, passing Natalia enroute from the kitchen to the bedroom she and Natalia shared. As usual, Natalia looked exquisite. But, of course, Natalia always did. Natalia's robe, knotted easily at her slender waist, was of pink silk, ever so slightly longer than ankle length so that, as Natalia walked, it looked perfectly natural for her to raise the hem slightly, pinching the fabric between the tips of her long fingers. There was a hint of white linen visible just above where the robe crossed over at the front.

"Would you like me to make you some tea or coffee or something, Annie?"

"Coffee'd be wonderful. I just have to change. I'll be out in a minute." Annie entered the bedroom. She could see Natalia's small suitcase, open on the floor beside the bed, the revolvers and gunbelt visible.

Before she changed, there was a more urgent need. She went to the bathroom . . .

Annie Rourke Rubenstein pulled her nightgown—it was ankle length with a ruffle at the hem, sleeveless and pale blue with a white ribbon which traversed the neckline and tied in a bow at the front—over her head. She put on her robe—it was of blue and pink wool plaid, very sensible looking and warm—then took up her brush and began to work it through her hair. She couldn't picture women envying her hair, as her mother had said. She'd always liked her hair, but thought it was pretty ordinary.

This whole "pajama party," as her mother, Sarah Rourke, kept referring to it, scared her. It was emotionally destructive to Maria Leuden. It was dangerous for Natalia, Annie thought, considering Natalia was still recovering from what could loosely be described as a nervous breakdown.

There were pills Natalia could take which would help her to relax. Doctor Rothstein, at Mid-Wake, had insisted Natalia have them available, these in addition to the subcutaneously planted timed release capsule inserted near Natalia's neck. Eventually, the capsule would be totally dissolved. It contained a drug Doctor Rothstein, the psychiatrist who had worked to help Natalia at Mid-Wake, had described as a natural tranquilizer produced by the body, rather like the opposite of adrenaline; "it'll release when Natalia's body requires it, just helping her to relax."

But even so—

Annie finished with her hair, finding a white ribbon which matched the ribbon at the neckline of her gown, tying the ribbon into her hair at the nape of the neck. A little touch up with the hair brush again.

She noticed her eyes in the mirror. There was something akin to a wariness in them.

She closed her eyes, just standing there holding the hair brush . . .

Sarah Rourke tied her robe over her bulging abdomen. She looked at

106

herself in the mirror as she began to brush her hair. She hadn't tried to make this a "bitch session," as Natalia had called it, but a help session. Maria Leuden was hopelessly in love with Michael—and hopeless seemed to be the operative word. Both she—Sarah—and Natalia were in love with the same man, Michael's and Annie's father, John.

But something else nagged at Sarah Rourke, and she would not even commit words to the thoughts, even in her mind. The thoughts frightened her . . .

The sixteen men, led by Hugo Goerdler, arrived at precisely eight-fifteen, Freidrich Rausch waiting in silence, camouflaged by the snow itself, the American M-16 rifle chambering the primitive cased ammunition cheeked close as they came.

He had to be certain that Goerdler and his men were, in fact, who they were supposed to be. There was much turmoil in New Germany and it was always possible that somehow the party had been penetrated and traced to the new headquarters in what had been Mexico, then a substitution made.

But as they approached and he momentarily exchanged the rifle for a pair of vision intensification binoculars, he was certain the sixteen were the right men.

Hugo Goerdler, Rausch's political superior in the SS and one of the few men Rausch felt was more deadly than he when needed—not in the sense of combat, but in the sense of creativity—moved at the head of the ragged column of snow-smocked figures, uniformed as commandoes of New Germany. This struck a note of humor in Freidrich Rausch, that they were disguised as men under the command of the despicable Wolfgang Mann, yet a note of irony as well. It was Hugo Goerdler who personally oversaw the assassination of Wolfgang Mann's wife in the streets of New Germany.

Rausch put down his snow splotched vision intensification binoculars and re-cheeked the rifle. "Hugo, my friend! I could have had you!"

Goerdler and his men looked up toward Rausch's position with the simultaneity of a well-rehearsed chorus line.

Goerdler shouted back, "Does that make us even now for the time I stole your pants, Freidrich?"

Freidrich Rausch laughed aloud, the laughter warming him as he signalled his lifelong friend forward . . .

* * *

"I was sorry, Freidrich, gravely sorry when I learned—"

"I shall avenge Damien. Then I can be sorry," Rausch said, looking into his hands for a moment, then taking a small sip from his flask. There were a series of tunnels within the construction, to be obliterated when Eden Base was completed. But for now, they housed the fifteen men who had accompanied Hugo Goerdler.

This particular tunnel, Rausch's home of late, was all to themselves.

"You have a plan, I take it, for killing this Rourke woman?"

"A very simple plan, really. But they are always the best, are they not, the simple ones?" He lit a cigarette, then blew smoke toward the map on the wall of the tunnel. "The Retreat of this Doctor Rourke. His wife, his daughter, the Russian woman who is said to be his mistress, even the mistress of his son—they are all there. And they have two radios, one as primary and one in the event the first fails. I have been assembling a low power transmitter from the Eden Project stores, one only powerful enough for the signal to travel a few miles within such high mountains, not powerful enough for the signal to be intercepted at Eden Base or by Mann—damn him—or any of his so-called commandoes. I have also constructed a second device, with which I can jam outgoing signals within an area of several miles, thus preventing the women from contacting Mann for aid. I will lure them out, since Damien was unable to leave specific details for me concerning the method of entry to this Retreat or I have been unable to discern such details. But I shall lure them out, then murder them. Then I will enter the Herr Doctor's Retreat and incinerate it. Rourke will be so obsessed with finding the killer of these four women—especially considering the manner in which they shall die—that he will not rest and, more importantly, he will be neutralized, so preoccupied he will not be able to adequately aid Mann and his forces, or foil our plans concerning New Germany and Eden."

"What of Commander Dodd?" Goerdler asked, then returning to chewing his rather small, almost childish looking lower lip. The lip distended, made him appear to be pouting. Now it was cracked from the cold.

"Dodd is an opportunist, Hugo. He will be our most loyal colleague until it is no longer in his best interests, then he will betray us. But until then, he can be useful. Once the day comes, I tell you, I will draw lots with you for the pleasure of killing him, eh?"

There was laughter in Goerdler's dark eyes. Some said that

Goerdler's physical features reminded them of photographs of Jews, but such persons who spoke such lies were to be counted among Hugo Goerdler's detractors. The fellow Rubenstein, who was the companion of Doctor Rourke, after all was a Jew, yet there were no distinguishing marks about his countenance, as much as Rausch had looked for them. One would be hard-pressed, at any event, to find anyone who more devoutly epitomized the goals of National Socialism than Hugo Goerdler.

Goerdler was fingering his brass identity disk, put it on the rough table and opened his own flask. "We will aid you, Freidrich, however you wish. You perform a task for all of New Germany, for the future of the race."

Freidrich Rausch raised his flask. "Heil Hitler," he whispered, the import of the centuries old toast swelling him with purpose, with pride. To follow one so glorious, so all-knowing and so selfless was a task and a joy, requiring total dedication of self, in spirit and body. To give less was treason and dishonor.

They touched their flasks together in silence, then the instant before they drank, Hugo Goerdler murmured the same words, "Heil Hitler."

They drank and then there was a long moment of silence . . .

"To happiness and peace," Annie said, raising her glass.

"Here, here," Sarah smiled.

Natalia raised her glass as well. "I echo Annie!"

Maria, silent, raised her glass and the four women drank, Natalia noticing all of them sipped at their drinks as did she. It would be a long night.

Earlier in the day, Annie had baked soda crackers and prettily arranged on the soda crackers were various bits of this and that, meat, fowl, even fresh fish brought from Mid-Wake. There was a dip, as well, and although Natalia wasn't quite sure what it contained, it tasted vaguely oniony and quite delicious. But she only sampled it, not really hungry.

"I didn't want this to be an unpleasant time for us," Sarah Rourke said. "But, well, I just thought we all needed to try to help each other to solve some of our problems. Maybe it was a bad idea."

"If Michael does not feel he should marry me, well, I will respect his judgment. That should be simple enough," Maria said, not looking at anyone, her hands in the pockets of her terrycloth robe. She wore pajamas, the only one of them who did. Natalia wondered if that were conscious—the "pajama party" image—or merely custom?

"That's your business, but Michael is my son, even if he is only a couple of years younger than I am. So, I guess I have a right to speak my mind. Well, maybe not a right, but a reason. I don't want to hurt you. It's just that I love you both, and I want you both to be happy." Sarah paused, then, voice low, added, "And I'm sure Madison would have wanted that, too."

Natalia said, "Madison was a very sweet girl. In that way, Maria, very much like you. You are both very different, however, and I think—and this is only opinion—that Michael was attracted to you because of your differences from Madison and the similarities, attracted to you as the whole person. With the passivity you seem to exhibit to Michael's will, I'm not sure you're doing him a service, or a service to yourself."

"Michael's too much like his father. I guess what worries me," Sarah said, retying the belt from her robe into a bow, "is that I made mistakes, John made mistakes. They hurt, mistakes do, and I don't wish any hurt to either of you."

Annie was sipping at her drink, looked over the rim of the glass as she spoke. "I like this evening better. Earlier, I didn't know what was happening, but I didn't like it at all. But I think we should make a ground rule. If someone doesn't want to discuss—well, talk about things like this, well, they can say that and the subject's off limits. Okay?"

"A good rule, Annie," Natalia agreed, doubting it would be adhered to despite the best intentions.

Yes," Sarah said. "Look—I'm feeling very guilty here, but I only wanted to help. I didn't want this to be unpleasant; maybe I'm just a fool."

"Frau—I mean Sarah—ahh, I know you are not a fool, that you are a good person who only wants the best for Michael and myself, and for Annie and Paul and Natalia, and for yourself and your husband," Maria said, at last smiling.

Sarah looked at her, an earnestness in her voice that Natalia could not deny. "If we can help each other, maybe gain some fresh insights. That's all I wanted."

"I don't think anything will really be resolved until there is a resolution to the war," Natalia interjected. "If you think about each of us, our

110

situation, everything is hinged on the war and always has been. Before the Night of the War, Sarah, you and John were putting your lives back together. He's told me." Sarah only nodded, looking down, as if studying the toe of her right slipper. "And if it weren't for the war, we wouldn't be co-existing now. We would have died—Sarah, Annie, myself—centuries before you were born, Maria. Sara and Annie and I would not be contemporaries. I would be living in Russia or still working in Latin America—"

"I might never have met Paul," Annie interrupted, then laughed, her eyes finally smiling. "I m horrible, but if this was the only way—but I would have been a little girl and he would have been an old man by the time I'd grown up."

"Michael would have been dead half a millenia ago," Maria said, almost bemused-sounding. "And if there had been a war later, and I had still been born and become an archeologist as I am, I might—" Her shoulders shook.

"I wonder if John would have made me pregnant," Sarah said suddenly. "I mean, for a while, I used to think that maybe he just got me pregnant to apologize for letting you—" She looked at Annie. "—and your brother grow up. But I don't think so, now. But, the baby—I would have never—"

Natalia stood up, placed her hands in the pockets of her robe, looked at Annie, Maria and Sarah in turn as she spoke. "I think the thing is that the war—for good and for bad—is the inescapable catalyst in all our lives, all our relationships." She reached down and took one of the non-carcinogenic German cigarettes from the table, lit it in the flame of her lighter, exhaled smoke as she continued to talk. "The war dominates life for us and will, as long as it goes on. We can say and do all we want, and there will be some changes; but, in the final analysis, none of the changes will make any real difference. We were all thrown together by this and until it's over, what can we do? I don't know." None of the other women spoke. "I'm going to bed. Maybe things will look different tomorrow, hmm?"

Natalia started for the bedroom.

But then the voice came over the radio.

Chapter Twenty-six

The wind blew cold and still heavier overcast of snow laden gray-black clouds was moving in rapidly from the north.

The green wash was long gone and, replacing it, was a very intense pain and cold, his body shivering and, each time a spasm came, the pain across his back that much more acute.

"I believe, Herr Lieutenant, that the bullet somehow damaged bone in your right shoulder blade. This is why, Herr Lieutenant, the pain is so intense."

Horst Hammerschmidt grimaced as another spasm came upon him, focusing his eyes and all his concentration on Sergeant Schlabrendorff's weathered face. "Casmir—I am giving you an order. Word must be gotten to the High Command concerning this new weapon we have witnessed. You will ride Rommel. Any radio transmissions might be intercepted. You must leave me and go at once."

"But, Herr Lieutenant!"

Snow fell into his eyelashes and he blinked it away, the spasm lasting longer than one had ever lasted before. But he could not show that to Schlabrendorff, for as much as his sergeant was the best of soldiers, his sergeant was also his friend, like a second father to him in many ways. If Casmir Schlabrendorff suspected that the pain was worsening, he might not leave. "It is also the best thing for me, Casmir. If you ride Rommel like the wind, you can be back for me with help in just a few days."

"Herr Lieutenant—there are—"

"There are too many excuses, Sergeant. You have your orders. Leave me with what supplies you can—" Most of their supplies, including the climate controlled tents which were used to survive the bitter cold of the night in these high altitudes, were lost, aboard pack animals at the rear of the column. "And as much ammunition as you can spare as well."

Casmir Schlabrendorff's always sad looking eyes seemed sadder now. He only nodded . . .

Rommel moved uneasily. If there were another man Hammerschmidt's horse was used to, it was Schlabrendorff, but Rommel was rarely ridden by anyone except Hammerschmidt, hadn't been for months.

Schlabrendorff looked uneasy in the saddle. Hammerschmidt called up to him from the improvised shelter beneath which he lay in the rocks high above any trail. "Remember, Casmir. Rommel will not fail you. Like you, he is a good German soldier." Horst Hammerschmidt forced a smile.

"I will return for you, Herr Lieutenant. I swear it." And Casmir Schlabrendorff pulled himself more erect in the saddle and saluted.

Pain washed over Hammerschmidt, nausea on its crest, faintness below the surface as he pushed himself up on his left elbow and raised his right hand, returning the salute. "I place my life, but, more importantly, the life of New Germany in your hands. I feel in perfect safety, Sergeant."

Hammerschmidt snapped down the salute as smartly as he could, Schlabrendorff doing the same.

"Like the wind, Herr Lieutenant. Like the wind." And Schlabrendorff, a fine horseman, drew in Rommel's reins more tightly for an instant as he wheeled the animal, then, Rommel rearing slightly, Schlabrendorff moved his knees, easing pressure on the reins. Rommel bounded away across the plateau. The flat rocky expanse right angled and stopped less than a mile distant, dropping down into a rough excuse for a trail leading downward. As Schlabrendorff rode off, Horst Hammerschmidt began to succumb to the pain, but he heard over the drumming of Rommel's hoofbeats, "Like the wind!"

Chapter Twenty-seven

John Thomas Rourke, his heavier winter gear left in an office provided for his use, was stripped down to black sweater, black BDU pants and the double Alessi shoulder holster for his twin stainless Detonics pistols. The only items of arctic clothing he still wore were the boots, and his feet felt heavy and warm inside them as he stood, arms crossed over his chest, at the foot of the hospital bed.

A German doctor, attending the man in the bed, was rousing the man gently. John Rourke, Michael and Paul all recognized the figure: Vassily Prokopiev, when last seen by any of them designated field commander for the KGB Elite Corps, a decent man with honor.

John Rourke wondered if honor was what had brought Prokopiev here, injured, recovering from frostbite, speaking out of his pain of some urgent message, brought John Rourke and his son and his friend as well.

Prokopiev's eyelids fluttered and his head moved, as if awakening from ordinary sleep. "Herr Doctor, I have administered a mild stimulant. He should be fully awake and able to converse in a matter of moments. He will still be quite weak and, drifting in and out as he has been, there is the significant likelihood that he may, to some degree or another, be rather incoherent."

"I'm aware of the possibilities, Doctor," John Rourke nodded to his fellow physician.

Michael sat down on the small chair nearest to the bed, Michael and Prokopiev friends of a sort, comrades in an experience in the Second Chinese City which John Rourke knew neither Michael nor the Soviet officer would be likely to ever forget. Because of that friendship, it would be best that Michael's face should be the first face Vassily Prokopiev would see.

"Little one—"

The German physician, still beside the bed on the side opposite from Michael, looked up and said, "He was discovered with a Wild Tribes child, the age nearly four years as best we can tell, but the child quite small, malnourished. It appears that the young man did his very best to keep the child alive, even at risk of his own life. He alternates between asking about the child and asking for you. Sometimes, he is quite lucid, sometimes not. The fever he had was very stubborn to combat, but he is progressing nicely now."

"And the child?" Paul asked.

"The child is well. A hardy little thing, certainly. There is, as yet, no idea what to do with her. It is assumed her parents are dead. Her skin is rough, a little leathery, but typical for the Wild Tribes people. She seems genetically normal, as are many of them from the Wild Tribes, usually the weaker ones."

"Little one—"

John Rourke watched Vassily Prokopiev's face intently. A Soviet officer of the Elite Corps, a message, protecting a child against God only knew what horrors before the Germans found him. What was he doing here?

Little one—"

Chapter Twenty-eight

Still in their nightclothes, Natalia and Annie and Maria huddled around the primary radio. As Natalia looked up, she could see Sarah returning from the storage area where the auxiliary radio was kept.

"He's speaking in German. It's clearer now. But the signal is so terribly weak. Before, I wasn't even sure of the language," Natalia declared. Then she looked at Maria Leuden. "You agree?"

"Yes. German, definitely. Perhaps a downed pilot?"

"That makes sense," Annie nodded.

"What do we do about it? I tried getting out on the second radio and there wasn't any luck. I can't tell if it's Soviet jamming or weather conditions or what; and I checked the antenna lead all the way until it disappeared into the access shaft," Sarah Rourke added.

Natalia looked at the radio again, her head starting to ache from straining to hear through the headset. "If the man on the other end of this transmission is a downed pilot, he's in trouble—or at least logic would make us assume that. With the cold outside, that could mean he's in danger of dying. On one hand, we have no choice but to go out and attempt to find him. And that shouldn't be that hard. I can adjust a walkie-talkie to the proper frequency and as the signal strength increases, we'll eventually find him. If he's getting through and we're unable to get out, he must be very close, despite the weak signal. He could be low on power. On the other hand, this could be some sort of ruse to get us out of the Retreat. It could be Rausch out there, waiting for us."

"We cannot leave the man—" Maria insisted.

"I know that," Natalia nodded. "This is your house, Sarah? What do you suggest?"

Sarah licked her lips. "Two go out and two stay. Annie and Maria can—"

"No, damnit!" Annie snapped. "Look—you are not wandering around climbing rocks in sub-zero temperatures with the baby. Natalia and I should go."

"She's right," Natalia nodded, standing up, smoothing her hair, the headphones playing havoc with it. "She is."

Sarah touched at her abdomen. "You're right. But I don't have to like it. You'll need a code phrase in case there's something wrong."

"Yes," Natalia almost whispered. She thought of the black jumpsuit hanging in the closet. If it belonged to some other Natalia, she hoped it fit anyway.

Chapter Twenty-nine

"Whatever you have to say, you can say to the three of us," John Rourke told Vassily Prokopiev. Prokopiev's eyes looked slightly glassy, but he sounded normal enough. Rourke had looked at his chart and supposed the glassiness was a result of medication. Five centuries ago, Vassily Prokopiev would have been dead, quite likely, or in the best case scenario have lost several limbs at a minimum. But treatment of frostbite and exposure-related injuries had advanced considerably. The prognosis on the chart was a good one for restoration to normal health.

Prokopiev nodded. His speech was a little slurred, but seemed otherwise lucid as he spoke. "I was called before the Comrade Marshal."

"Antonovitch?" John Rourke and Paul Rubenstein queried almost in unison.

"He spoke to me of his desire to end war, at first end war with war, but how then he had realized that his desire could not be fulfilled as he had originally hoped, that instead there would be the destruction of mankind."

"What—" Michael began.

John Rourke told his son, "Let him finish, Michael."

Prokopiev nodded again. "Particle Beam technology. The Comrade Marshal told me that it is so advanced now that the Particle Beam weapons can be mounted in helicopter gunships, on tanks, made in whatever size or power range is needed, even as machine guns for the infantry."

Rourke shivered as Prokopiev went on, in his mind seeing Reed as the Army Intelligence officer had climbed the masts for the Particle Beam Weapons at the Soviet Womb in Colorado, with his dying breath trying to raise the American flag in a symbol of defiance. "The Comrade Marshal told me that no power on earth would be able to stand against these Particle Beam devices except by use of nuclear weapons. In New Germany nuclear weapons are under development. There is still the Chinese nuclear arsenal somewhere out there and the Soviet community beneath the sea has such weapons as well. Once the new Particle Beam weapons are used in the field, nuclear weapons will be used against them and this will bring the end of mankind.

"The Comrade Marshal," Prokopiev went on slowly, "gave to me a small cannister, so small that it is little larger than a spool of thread. There is film contained inside that cannister which has the plans for the Particle Beam devices. I am to give this film to you. He told me that he trusted that you will do the right thing with it. I am to tell Major Tiemerovna a message as well, that the Comrade Marshal says she was right about him after all, that he was not born to Karamatsov's work. And I am to tell you, Doctor Rourke, that he believes that this changes nothing between you and him. He would kill you if he had the chance and—I quote him—'I will expect the same courtesy from him.'"

John Rourke leaned heavily against the hard plastic footboard of the bed. "You don't have this capsule anymore, do you?"

"It is in the half-track truck. It was safer there. The child—You understand."

"Yes. You must tell us, Vassily, where this truck can be located. We must find the capsule and I must get its contents to allied scientists in the hopes that we can somehow find a defense, even if it means crafting these weapons ourselves."

Prokopiev looked tired and weak. His voice sounded very old as he said, "I will need a map, Doctor."

Chapter Thirty

Annie Rourke Rubenstein had always felt awkwardly unfeminine wearing trousers or pants of any kind and avoided them with a passion; but logic dictated the heavy arctic weight snow pants because of the severe cold. Annie had learned to listen to her own logic, so she wore them. She supposed that, to a large part, the aversion she felt was psychological, with just her brother and herself growing up alone in the Retreat after their father had returned to the Sleep.

John Rourke had spent five years with them in intensive tutoring for their survival and their abilities to educate themselves. Yet there were other necessities, among these a conscious need to assert her femininity within the larger framework of personality development. There were no girl friends with whom to share secrets and experiences, no older women to whom she could go for advice. She had to construct her own role through trial and error, find a lynchpin for her concept of self. She remembered her father telling them once, "No matter how much you know, you will never fully know yourself; no matter how much you learn, if you ever consider your education completed you'll have learned nothing. Learning to know yourself is the ultimate discipline."

But she had to maintain her own identity separate from that of her brother. And, as a constant reminder of her sex, there were the cryogenically sleeping role models of her mother, Sarah Rourke, and Natalia, tantalizingly near, yet unable to be confided to, questioned, imitated.

Their nights alone in the Retreat—hers and Michael's—would be spent in various pursuits: books, music, videos, chess, physical fitness. But there were other needs, to make, to do. Michael would work with guns and radios and machinery. Although Annie could detail strip a .45 automatic or a Colt assault rifle as quickly and well as he, and knew basic maintenance for the equipment housed at the Retreat, she had taught herself other things to pass the time profitably: dressmaking, knitting, crocheting, and hence design. The clothes she made were not only for herself, but for her brother—a shirt, a sweater. Her father had planned ahead, laying in the supplies women would need to make clothing, for crafts. Sometimes when she thought about it, she smiled, imagining her plus-six-foot father, his twin Detonics .45s under his battered old leather bomber jacket, going into a fabric store and purchasing material, yarn, thread, embroidery floss, even the sewing machine housed at the Retreat (along with, of course, a spare parts kit and detailed maintenance manuals).

They would work their garden plots in the months—precious few—which passed for a growing season during those years. But in the winter months with time in the out-of-doors cut back, her "hobbies" or "life skills" (depending on how they were perceived) became all that much more consuming, and symbolic of her own identity.

As she and Natalia stepped into the frigid blasts just beyond the Retreat's exterior door, Annie drew the scarf layered over the toque which already covered her face still tighter. And she was glad she'd heeded that little voice of logic again.

It had been hard waiting, doing the necessary things while the voice of the injured man droned on over the radio, begging for help. Internal injuries, dizziness. The cold.

But if she and Natália were to have any hope of reaching him and any hope of getting back to the Retreat, not to mention insuring themselves as much as possible against the possibility of a trap, the time in preparation had to be spent. While Natalia worked to change two of the walkie-talkies to the appropriate frequency for the downed pilot's broadcast, with her mother helping, Annie quickly field stripped and cleaned the firearms they would take with them, insuring that the lubrication was sparingly applied, that any gummy residues which could turn to sludge in such cold were scrubbed away with added care beyond the usual. Maria packed for them small rucksacks that contained emergency medical supplies, lightweight insulating blankets, even some food, just in case.

As the main entrance to the Retreat closed behind them, despite

Natalia's presence, Annie had never felt more isolated, because the darkness was so unremitting, the swirl of snow around them like a giant dust devil or tornado, the wind so strong she could barely stand against it. And she felt as if the very elements surrounded her, shielded her from contact with any fellow human being.

She tried to force the thoughts from her head, telling herself that she should concentrate on the mission, finding and saving this downed German pilot who made such plaintive appeals over the radio for assistance.

But when she thought of the mission, the sense of isolation became comingled with foreboding.

Chapter Thirty-one

Snow beat almost malevolently against the vision-corrected armored glass. Once it accumulated where the wiper blades could not reach it and to such an extent that the convection heating system wired into the glass itself could not instantly melt it away, the magnified crystalline geometric shapes were almost touchingly beautiful.

The vehicle, in which they traversed the land that had so often served as inhospitable host to warring armies over the generations, was as yet un-designated, so many changes made in its design during prototyping and pre-production, yet the urgency of getting into the field so great for the German war machine, that it was merely called the Armored, All-Terrain, Severe Atmospheric Conditions Vehicle. With the German penchant for complex naming—a helicopter could be called "a machine which screws itself into the air"—John Rourke thought the ungainly name might stick. So Rourke merely labelled it with the equally awkward acronym the first letters of the English translation made—AATSACV. He pronounced it "Atsack."

The Atsack, fitted with all-side sensors and heads-up display in the cocoonable windshield for enhanced navigational abilities, piloted well. Because of the truly gigantic (three meters in height), independently suspended tires, the Atsack actually moved more rapidly and smoothly than Rourke would have thought possible for something of such considerable size. It was roughly twice the size of the motor homes made by firms like Winnebago before the Night of The War. No color television or VCR, he reflected, smiling, as he looked over Michael's shoulder, Michael at the Atsack's controls. But there was the modern incarnation of a microwave oven, for heating rations.

It buzzed now and Rourke moved along the Atsack's deck despite the ruggedness of the terrain, the self-compensating, computer controlled suspension giving him an environment steady and level enough in which delicate surgery could have been performed. With the heat turned to a comfortable level, he and Paul and Michael could move about in shirt sleeves. He took the hot soup from the microwave, setting it on the counter, beginning to consume it as he marshalled his thoughts.

He could frequently think more clearly while thinking of several things at once, so, while he ate, his eyes scanned the pages of one of the technical manuals for the Atsack, the German, because it was so technical, difficult for him to read, in a curious way almost heightening his abilities to focus a portion of his concentration in other directions.

Namely the Particle Beam technology.

Antonovitch's remarks to Vassily Prokopiev, however apocalyptic, might well prove to be a conservative estimate of the situation which was emerging. If the land-based Soviets could, through use of this superior technology, make their armies into an all-but-invincible juggernaut and this were backed up by the seapower of the historic enemies of Mid-Wake, with their submarine based thermonuclear missiles as the trump card, the Germans would have no choice but to use defensive nuclear capabilities currently under development—if there was the time.

But as few as one or two nuclear detonations above ground could destroy the already fragile nuclear envelope, precipitating the end of life on the surface forever, the end of mankind.

All hopes, all dreams, everything.

John Rourke put down the soup spoon.

Chapter Thirty-two

Natalia Anastasia Tiemerovna turned her face away from the wind and adjusted both the black silk scarves over her face and head and the silk toque beneath them, repositioning her snow goggles as well, then pulling the snorkel hood more tightly closed at the front of her face. It had the effect of tunnel vision, but there was no choice.

As she walked, bent against the wind, Annie beside her, she dug in the climbing staff she carried. After only five minutes, the visibility so terrible, the wind so strong, she had decided that their only safe course of action was to tie themselves together, which they did.

The clothing they wore was such that she could be exposed to the temperature extreme around them for quite some time without feeling ill-effects, at least theoretically. She was beginning to doubt the theory.

The fronts of her thighs, her forehead, her feet and hands were all starting to feel stiff with the cold and wind and, as they walked, she made a decision. If the downed pilot could not be located within the next ten minutes, they would turn back.

It would be that or lose their own lives.

She had not yet mentioned her decision to Annie. There had been no opportunity to speak, normal speech impossible because of the high-pitched shrieking of the wind through each crevice and niche of rocks, through the snow-buried boughs of the pines. To speak and be heard, it would be necessary to push back one's parka hood and remove at least one facial covering and almost touch one's mouth to the other person's ear, then shout.

Natalia kept moving instead.

The road leading up and down from the Retreat's main entrance was what they followed now and had followed since leaving, logic dictating that if the downed airman's craft had landed too far away from the road they would not hear him at all because no craft could have survived the crash.

But there were flatter, more level spaces to the side of the road nearer to the base of the mountain, the places where five centuries ago the Soviet aircraft under the command of Rozhdestvenskiy had landed KGB Elite Corps troops in an effort to locate and destroy the Retreat before the fires swept the sky.

It was here, in once wooded meadows now feet deep with snow, that the downed pilot would have attempted to land, and toward this area that they walked.

They crossed up into a small, more level expanse of the road, the snow less deep here, the walking, by comparison, easier, but the wind stronger and Natalia instantly felt colder.

But she smiled. It felt good to be in action again, although she doubted Doctor Rothstein at Mid-Wake would have agreed.

She looked to her pistol belt, the snow which had accumulated on the flaps of her holsters nearly blown away by the stronger wind here. Annie beside her, she kept walking.

As the road began to angle downward again, she felt Annie tug at the rope. Natalia looked toward her, saw her gesturing out beyond the road. And Natalia's eyes followed in the direction toward which Annie pointed.

Two hundred yards away, in one of the flat expanses where five centuries ago Soviet gunships had landed, there was a German gunship now, all but burned beyond recognition, merely a skeleton remaining.

Natalia nodded, shifting her M-16 forward, hoping it would still work as they started down from the road, toward the wreck.

Chapter Thirty-three

Michael Rourke saw the truck, a Soviet half-track, almost wholly buried in snow, wedged against jagged outcroppings of almost black looking granite, the rocks themselves what had saved the truck from being totally obscured by the snow.

He shifted his shoulder beneath his parka under the weight of the double shoulder holster for his Berettas, his eyes through his snow goggles scanning the ground in an attempt to find a passage at once safe and convenient between his present location above the truck and the truck itself. He could always double back, and was not willing to risk a broken leg or worse simply to save a few minutes in reaching the truck.

But he saw a sort of path, drifted over high with snow, so its actual outline and depth were in doubt. If he were cautious it would be worth a try and there would be minimal risk.

Michael Rourke opened the velcro closure of one of his parka's side pockets and spoke into the small short-range German handset which he extracted from it. "This is Hunter Three calling Hunter One and Hunter Two. Are you reading me? This is Hunter Three calling Hunter One and Hunter Two. Do you read? Over."

"This is Hunter One, reading you loud and clear. I've just rendez-voused with Hunter Two. Over."

"Hunter One. I have found the quarry. I say again. Have found the quarry. Do you Roger that? Over."

"Hunter Three, I Roger that. Good work. Leave your transmission open and we will close with your position. Do you Roger that? Over."

"I Roger that, Hunter One. Wilco. Hunter Three Out."

Michael Rourke slipped the radio handset back into the parka pocket and closed the flap, but the radio was still set to broadcast and its signal could be used by his father, Hunter One, and his brother-in-law, Hunter Two, to home in on him.

He shifted the M-16 rearward, positioning it diagonally across his back left shoulder to right hip on its sling now. Both hands might be needed and there was no sign, for as far as he could see, of human life. The four-inch barreled Model 629 was holstered accessibly enough at his waist in a flap holster which completely cocooned it and the knife old Jon the Swordmaker had given him, copied after the Crain Life Support System I, which five centuries ago had been the original basis for the LS-X, was at his hip as well, even more accessible than the revolver.

As Michael started picking his way through the drifts along what he hoped, indeed, was a navigable path, he recalled the story his father had told him concerning the origins of the heroically proportioned Life Support System-X. His father, John Rourke, and the Weatherford, Texas knifemaker, Jack Crain, were friends. Not really that long before The Night of The War, while John Rourke completed his work to fit and stock the Retreat, the conversation between John Rourke and his friend took place. They discussed a knife of the same basic design as the Life Support System I, but larger, not just a longer blade, proportionately larger so the knife wouldn't just be bigger, but of superior strength and mass and serviceability.

Originally, John Rourke had planned to carry this knife himself.

But, as fathers will, Michael's father had told him, he had instead put it away for his son to some day use. Unwittingly, when old Jon the Swordmaker gave him — Michael — the Life Support System I, it freed John Rourke of the unspoken promise to his son. Because of the ferocity of close combat at times, John Rourke had often considered using the knife but had never done so. With Michael possessed of a blade, though slightly smaller (three inches shorter in the blade and reduced overall dimensions), essentially equal, John Rourke decided to employ the blade himself. He said, "Some day, it can be for your son."

Michael halved the distance between the rocky outcropping from which he'd first seen the Soviet half-track truck and the truck itself.

The snow was deeper than he'd anticipated and the going slower, drifts well above his waist, the only means of locomotion at all practical for Michael Rourke to work his way along the rocks flanking the path virtually hand over hand, raising his legs as high as he could, lurching ahead and downward.

He slipped, falling full into the snow, half-burying himself within it, "swimming" out of it and to his feet. He brushed the snow away from his goggles and as much as he could from the flap holster and his knife.

He started along the path again, a two foot square patch of the truck's cab and a six foot or so square patch of the vehicle's left side all that guided him.

There was a bend in the path and, despite his exhaustion from the struggle of merely trying to walk and his eagerness to reach the truck, he stopped, assessing what might possibly lie around the bend.

There were still no signs of footprints or vehicle treads anywhere visible around the area. But with the velocity of the wind and the volume of the snowfall, such traces would obliterate almost instantly.

Michael Rourke swung the M-16 forward, brushing snow from the closed dust cover, from the trigger guard. He didn't remove the rubberized muzzle plug since he could shoot through that if necessary and accumulating snow down the bore would pose a worse threat of obstruction.

His gloved fist on the Colt assault rifle's pistol grip, his right thumb poised at the selector, Michael Rourke started forward.

As he reached the spot where the rugged track he followed took an almost unnaturally sharp right angle, he leaned forward, the muzzle of the M-16 going ahead of him.

Michael Rourke's wrist almost snapped as whatever it was—a blur of grayish-white against the snow and the darkness—impacted the M-16 at the carrying handle, the pistol grip slipping from his momentarily numbed fingers, hands—they were gloved in discolored brownish pink leather—tearing at the rifle. But the rifle was still slung to him crossbody and Michael was dragged forward.

As he fell, his right hand reached for the revolver, but his fingers still couldn't close. His left hand went out ahead of him, fingers splayed, palm flat as he plowed into and through the snow, something ripping at the sling, twisting it, the sling biting deep into the left side of his neck.

Michael tried pulling away, got to his left knee, reached for the sling with both hands. As he looked up, he saw the face which belonged to the gloved hands. And he saw the hands more closely.

The hands were half-gloved, half-wrapped in human skin and the face was nearly obscured in a frozen mat of beard and eyebrows and long hair which almost hooded the head, eyes glowing out at him from the center. As Michael twisted at the sling, something impacted his right arm and he fell left, realizing as he fell that not his arm had been struck, but the rifle stock. A club—it was a human femur—swung through the air and downward toward him.

Michael let himself fall, the pain at the left side of his neck where the sling pressured against him excruciating. He told himself he'd lived through worse as his left hand found the butt of the knife made for him by old Jon the Swordmaker. He ripped it from the leather and arced it left to right, slicing through the tensioned web fabric sling, his body falling all the way back now that he was free of it, the femur passing inches from his eyes and nose.

He slipped back through the snow, down along the rocky defile which had been his path to the Soviet half-track truck, spreading his arms and legs to slow himself, feeling returning to his right wrist and hand, with it pain.

The second neanderthal-like man—he was a Wild Tribesman, obviously one of those who had turned to cannibalism for survival—threw himself forward, diving, impacting the snow inches from Michael as Michael skidded into a wall of granite, his left shoulder impacting it hard. He nearly lost the knife.

The Wild Tribesman was to his feet, the first one running through the snow as if it weren't there, he moved so quickly. Michael's right hand worked well enough and he reached to the flap holster at his side, tearing open the closure, his fingers clutching for the rubber grips. As the first Wild Tribesman—now brandishing the M-16, but inverted, holding it by the muzzle to use as a club—came within striking range, Michael had the four-inch barreled .44 Magnum clear of the leather, firing it from chest height, double actioning it once, then once more, then again, all three 180-grain jacketed hollow points connecting; he could see the bits of ragged military uniforms and pelts of human flesh covering the Wild Tribesman spraying away under the impacts.

Man followed gun, the M-16's butt plowing into the snow, the Wild Tribesman's face and torso just after it.

As Michael Rourke wheeled to take the second man, something hit him from the left, the full force of another human body, a third Wild Tribesman crashing down on him from the rocks against which Michael had impacted seconds earlier.

Michael's revolver discharged, the second Wild Tribesman's human bone club flying upward into the snow, lost in the darkness as the bullet hit the Wild Tribesman's right shoulder. Michael Rourke fell back, sprawling into the snow, but still clutching his knife.

The Wild Tribesman who had tackled him tackled him again, Michael rolling across the snow with him, the man's weight crushingly heavy as they stopped, Michael beside the edge of the pathway downward toward the truck, the Wild Tribesman's snarling face over his, the Wild Tribesman's right knee on Michael's left forearm, pinning the knife down as well. Michael smashed upward with his right elbow, contacting bone, the Wild Tribesman rolling off him, but Michael's right arm numb.

To his feet, regrasping the knife old Jon had made for him.

The Wild Tribesman, from beneath a ragged Soviet arctic parka, likely the "skin" of a former prey, drew two Soviet Elite Corps bayonets, charging toward Michael now, both bayonets held clumsily like daggers.

Michael Rourke ducked left and down, slicing the knife in his hand through a snowdrift, scooping snow onto the blade flat, hurtling the snow into the face of his attacker. The Wild Tribesman's head snapped back and his eyes blinked. Michael lunged into a half-right turn, his knife held like a rapier, stabbing toward the carotid artery of the Wild Tribesman. The Wild Tribesman's right shoulder flexed and Michael's knife deflected across the shoulder muscles and over the uppermost right side of the back. The Wild Tribesman spun toward him, driving both bayonets downward. Michael dropped, rolled left, his legs scissoring outward and around the right leg of the Wild Tribesman. There was a snapping sound in the cold air, the Wild Tribesman's right leg caving in as a hideous scream issued from his lips.

Michael rolled away, the Wild Tribesman throwing his body mass toward Michael, both bayonets driving downward.

Michael Rourke came up to his right knee, lunging forward with the full extent of his left arm, driving the copy of the five centuries old Life Support knife edge upward into the Wild Tribesman's groin, then letting his own body weight drag the blade upward until it locked against bone.

Michael rolled left as the Wild Tribesman collapsed, blood geysering from the arteries Michael's weapon had severed.

Michael breathed. There was a sound half like a snarl, half like a scream. To his left. The Wild Tribesman he'd wounded, the one who'd been coming at him with the human bone club, charging toward him now, barehanded, right arm limp at his side.

They were evenly matched, the Wild Tribesman and Michael Rourke's right arms both useless to them. To his feet. The Wild Tribesman came like some charging locomotive. Michael edged back. There was no time for a weapon. As the Wild Tribesman threw himself toward Michael, Michael wheeled right in the trampled flat snow, his left leg rising, his numb right arm going out for balance, his left foot impacting the Wild Tribesman against the already injured right arm. The Wild Tribesman screamed.

As the Wild Tribesman stumbled, nearly past Michael, Michael finished the turn he'd started, the Wild Tribesman reeling, Michael Rourke jumping upward, drop kicking the Wild Tribesman in the injured right shoulder and right side of the chest, Michael's body vibrating with the impact. Michael fell. The Wild Tribesman swayed like an axed-through tree, then fell away, over the side of the path, in the next instant the sound of safety glass shattering.

The Wild Tribesman had impacted the cab of the Soviet half-track truck below.

Michael Rourke lay there for an instant, catching his breath, sweat bathing his body beneath the arctic gear, suddenly freezing cold.

His right arm was still numb.

Despite the cold, Michael opened his parka enough to access the Beretta 92F under his right armpit with his left hand, snapping it free, thumbing up the ambidextrous safety.

To his feet. He stumbled, caught himself.

Things to do. Close the parka. Check the other two, making certain, although there was little doubt about the one with the knife in his crotch.

His father and Paul would be coming, might have heard the sounds of the fight over the open radio transmitter in his right outside pocket—unless it was smashed. But they would have heard the sound of the gunfire at any event.

And so would any Russian patrols in the area.

Michael moved toward the edge of the path and looked downward. He could see the legs of the Wild Tribe cannibal, twisted, protruding upward through the cab of the half-track truck.

He spotted his revolver in the snow and started toward it.

Michael Rourke reached the revolver. Shivering now, he placed the Beretta under his limp right arm, caught up the revolver, shook some of the snow free from it, then thrust it into his belt. Again, he regrasped the Beretta.

The next task was the M-16.

But that was higher up along the trail.

He started to look for it, knowing that if he didn't keep moving until the sweat dried gradually from body heat, he stood a chance of freezing to death. Michael Rourke kept moving.

Chapter Thirty-four

The man from the charred helicopter was little more than a boy, a lieutenant in Wolfgang Mann's command by the uniform insignia he wore. But the head wound was so severe that Annie marveled at the fact he'd been able to make the transmission at all. She said as much to Natalia, kneeling there beside her in the meager shelter of the gunship as they fought to stabilize his condition to the point where it might be possible to get him back to the facilities at the Retreat, and there, just perhaps, save his life.

"He didn't make the transmissions. I'd be willing to bet on that," Natalia said, keeping her voice so low that Annie could barely hear her over the keening of the wind. "This is a trap. He is real, all right, and the injuries certainly are. But there's something wrong, Annie."

Annie Rourke Rubenstein looked around them. There were no signs of booby traps in the wrecked gunship, but that could have meant there really were some. There had been no footprints outside the machine, but with the blowing and drifting of the snow, any such markings would have been erased within seconds of being made.

"Are you sure?"

"I've seen enough head injuries in my life to know this man couldn't have been talking on the radio. This head wound would have made him unconscious—like he is now—instantly. Someone else sent the transmission and left this poor man here for us to find so everything would look genuine."

"To get us out here? But why not—"

"Strike now?" Natalia looked up from her work. "Whoever it is, wants all of us. That means getting inside the Retreat."

"But we can't not take him back. He'd die. What'll we do, Natalia?"

"I'm working on that," Natalia answered. Annie could see her eyes smiling where the snow goggles were pulled down. And Annie Rourke drew her M-16 closer to her before continuing to dress the shrapnel

134

wound in the man's left shoulder . . .

John Rourke stood beside his son as Paul walked back from the Soviet half-track truck, the location Vassily Prokopiev had given for the
capsule containing the data on the Particle Beam technology quite specific. Paul opened his gloved right hand and John Rourke opened his,
the capsule dropping from one hand to the other.

"How do we read this?" Michael asked, Rourke glancing at him. Michael was rubbing his right arm near the wrist. After as thorough an
examination as circumstances allowed under such severe weather conditions, John Rourke was quite confident there was no serious damage.

"I'd think it's some sort of microfilm, possible microdots. In either
case, we should be able to find a means of reading aboard the Atsack.
Which is the next order of business, gentlemen," Rourke said, looking
at his son and at his friend. John Rourke slung his M-16 slightly forward as he secured the capsule carefully into an inner pocket of his
parka. "If anything happens on the way, this has to get through to New
Germany and to Mid-Wake.

"Why both?" Paul asked. "For the obvious reason?"

And John Rourke smiled, nodded. "If they both have it, neither one
will have the edge. I don't want to have one war lead us into another.
Come on." And he pulled up the snow goggles as he tightened the snorkel hood closer about his face.

Chapter Thirty-five

There seemed to be two classes of these J7-V aircraft, Jason Darkwood noted, and this was evidently one from the luxury class. Colonel Mann's J7-V had a full bathroom, everything included, even a small stall-type shower, much like those on Soviet Scout Class submarines.

Jason Darkwood, the pain in his head and neck throbbing only moderately, took the container of pills given him by Doctor Munchen and opened it. He was to take one every four hours and have the prescription renewed at New Germany. And yes, Doctor Munchen had told him, the drug they contained reacted with adrenaline, in some patients more than others; but, the reaction was not harmful. Jason Darkwood also realized that there were two definitions of the word "harmful." To him, as a Fleet Officer in the United States Navy, a little pain was better than a lot of impaired judgment and a nervous reaction which prohibited normal activity.

He spilled the contents of the bottle into the chemical toilet and flushed it. He looked at himself in the mirror, noticed he was smiling.

Jason Darkwood felt better already . . .

Otto Hammerschmidt realized he was faced with the horns of the proverbial dilemma. He was a captain. He played chess with the ranking field grade commander in all of New Germany, Colonel Wolfgang Mann. There were general staff personnel, of course, but they never ventured into the field. The dilemma was that he could checkmate Colonel Mann on the next move.

"And what are you waiting for, Captain?"

Hammerschmidt looked up. "Herr Colonel?"

"Do you have so little respect for me, Hammerschmidt?"

Otto Hammerschmidt replied, "I have the greatest respect for you,

136

Herr Colonel. You are the finest officer under whom I have ever served or could hope to serve."

"Well, then?"

Hammerschmidt shrugged his shoulders—"Checkmate, Herr Colonel."—and moved the white queen . . .

Horst Hammerschmidt remembered the time he and his older brother, Otto, had run afoul of three boys in the Youth. The boys, schoolmates of Otto's, had pressed after Otto for several months to join and abandon his school athletics. It was because Otto was so good in intramural sports that it was not compulsory for him to join the Youth. Horst Hammerschmidt had perfected his athletic abilities so he could achieve the same exemption.

In those days, there had been no question—at least among the younger people of New Germany—to the leader's near infallibility and the preeminence of Nazism over all other philosophies, had any others even been openly available for study. But the Youth were fanatics, many of them.

The three boys had followed Otto and Horst home from a track competition in which older and younger boys were competing. Horst had competed in the triple broad jump, the 220 and the 440, not against his brother, but against students his own age and year. Otto was master of the 220, but excelled equally at the mile and the high jump.

On the way toward the main entrance to the city from the playing field, the three boys from the Youth had intercepted them. Their leader, Hugo Goerdler, an older boy who, it was said, worked with the Youth simply to satisfy his unnatural sexual appetites, insisted then and there that Otto and Horst quit athletics and join the Youth.

Otto's word was law with Horst then, the beginnings of the respect he had always held for his older brother. Otto had looked at him. Then Otto looked at Hugo Goerdler. "I will not, Hugo. Nor will my brother, Horst. Now, leave us."

That was when the fight began.

Hugo Goerdler stepped back and told the other two boys to show the Hammerschmidt brothers the error of their ways.

Despite the fact that the Youth boys carried clubs made from heavy sticks, the Hammerschmidt brothers prevailed.

Then Otto turned to Hugo Goerdler, who stood there, almost paralyzed with fear. Otto said to him, "Fight me, Hugo."

"I will not fight you."

Otto walked up to Hugo Goerdler, wiping blood from his lower lip where one of the stick clubs wielded by the two Youth boys had connected. Otto punched Hugo Goerdler in the mouth. It was a fast uppercut and knocked Hugo Goerdler flat on his rear end. As Hugo Goerdler fell back into the grass, he began to cry. Otto hauled Hugo Goerdler to his feet. Goerdler begged for mercy. Otto told Goerdler, "If you ever bother my brother or me again, I will beat you until you have no tears left. Remember that." And Otto let go of Hugo Goerdler's uniform front and let Goerdler fall back into the grass.

It had been warm in the sun as Horst Hammerschmidt and his big brother, Otto, walked home together, exchanging anecdotes about the fist fight, singing each other's fighting skills, laughing—but a little hollowly as Horst Hammerschmidt remembered it now—at the tragically pathetic character of Hugo Goerdler.

Horst Hammerschmidt's mind focused on that warm spring sunshine of years ago.

Because he was dying now, freezing to death . . .

Jason Darkwood was in dress blues. He remembered Maggie Barrow, when she'd helped him pack, telling him, "What are you going to need dress blues for?"

"A Fleet Grade officer may be called upon—"

"Oh, well, excuse me, Captain, sir!" And she saluted him. She looked kind of funny saluting him because she was wearing one of his shirts and nothing else. They'd just made love, for the first time in a long time. In a way, Jason Darkwood wondered if that was part of what had unnerved him. Had she made love to him because she thought she'd never see him again, as a parting gift?

He had to find out, because if she hadn't, he wanted to convert some of his United States Savings Bonds into cash and help her to start a civilian practice at Mid-Wake. Married women could serve in the Navy—as doubtless Maggie would as a Reserve Officer—but not sea duty.

He loved her.

He straightened his tie as the fuselage door opened.

He stood.

Colonel Mann, his cap at a slightly jaunty angle, Otto Hammerschmidt, the epitome of spit and polish, Sam Aldridge, boots shined to mirror brightness—Jason Darkwood stepped up to stand beside Colonel Mann. They were of equal rank, but Darkwood stood to the left.

He recognized the song being played by the military band. And he had spotted the counter-snipers surrounding the air field as they'd taxied.

The song was Deutschland Uber Alles . . .

The meal, veal, vegetables, pasta, things Jason Darkwood couldn't even recognize added in for good measure, was beyond the point of satisfying, nearly orgasmic.

Now, smoking cigars, along with Colonel Mann, Sam Aldridge and Otto Hammerschmidt and a rather unprepossessing older fellow named Deiter Bern, Jason Darkwood sat in a beautifully panelled library. Paneling was a novelty to him—real paneling—because at Mid-Wake, there was no wood of course.

A knock came at the doors and Colonel Mann turned toward it, as did Deiter Bern, the headman of New Germany, Darkwood unsure of his proper title beyond "Doctor."

A junior grade officer, uniform creases sharp enough to cut a tough shark steak, entered the room, saluted Colonel Mann (despite the fact both were uncovered) and even bowed slightly.

Colonel Mann returned the salute, took the message handed to him and read it.

Then he walked over to Otto Hammerschmidt. He spoke in English, Darkwood realized out of politeness. "Your brother, Otto, he may be gravely injured. Sergeant Schlabrendorff, whom I believe you know, has just arrived at one of our distant mountain outposts with reports of an attack by the Soviets utilizing some type of energy weapon. An expedition is being mounted even now to reach your brother. You would care to go, of course?"

"Yes, Herr Colonel."

Otto Hammerschmidt looked halfway between death and tears . . .

Jason Darkwood's dress blues would need attending to. There had been no time to hang them up, simply change to battle gear—black BDUs—and grab his weapons and move to the waiting helicopter gunship.

And they were off.

Trees, everywhere beneath them, a veritable Biblical Garden of Eden.

And, he now understood now why the surface dwellers fought as fiercely as they did.

The surface was Paradise.

The story of the Garden of Eden had not been apocryphal, but instead a prediction, a prediction not of the Fall that had been, but the Fall to come. The Night of the War was the Fall. And now, desperately, men were trying to reclaim their heritage, their future too.

Paradise was worth dying for.

Chapter Thirty-six

Paul Rubenstein sat at the main control panel of the Atsack, snow falling so thickly the wiper blades and defrosting system could barely keep pace in providing acceptable visibility.

Michael came forward and stood beside him. "Want me to spell you for a while?"

The Atsack was lumbering over a ridgeline toward a plateau they'd crossed enroute to the area where Vassily Prokopiev had told them he'd wrecked the Soviet half-track truck. The snow was deeper, of course, and the erratic winds altered the drift pattern. Because of that and the inherent ruggedness of the terrain, it was necessary to constantly monitor the headsup display showing computer translated readouts from the all-side sensors. Despite the comparatively enormous wheel size and base, the Atsack could get stuck. And no group of human beings, no matter how resourceful or physically strong, could ever hope to push it out without mechanical aid.

"Paul—you want me to—"

"Yeah—as soon as we get someplace where it'd be safe to change hands on the controls."

Michael leaned over Paul's shoulder. "Can you talk?"

"Sure. What's up?"

"There were a series of microdots. Dad's got them under a microscope now. Seems to be a full set of plans for both the Particle Beam weapons themselves and the power source."

"Great. At least we'll have what they have."

And then Paul heard John's voice behind him. "Not that great. I don't think it's intentional, probably simply because Antonovitch didn't have enough scientific training to realize. I can barely read the materials. But it seems that the system for linking the power to the weapon in such a way that there isn't instantaneous discharge—which would atomize the weapon and anything or anyone anywhere near it—it seems that that was omitted. We're going to need to get

141

our hands on one of the guns themselves in order to make a working prototype from these plans, unless the scientists of New Germany or Mid-Wake are a good deal farther advanced than available data suggests."

"Shit," Paul observed. The ridgeline was levelling out onto the plateau, and he could already envision himself getting out from behind the Atsack's controls for a while. He was starting to get a headache. "How do we get one of the guns? Why did I ask that?"

He heard John Rourke laughing behind him.

Michael said, "Well, the obvious thing that suggests itself is stealing one, right?"

John answered, the laughter gone from his voice, replaced by a timbre which suggested some difficulty in speaking, as if emotion were bottled up behind the words. "Logically, I'd suppose what we saw at that Wild Tribes relocation village was a field test for one of the weapons. Before World War Two, gas was tested on defenseless Ethiopians. The Spanish Civil War was in many ways a proving ground for Hitler—the Condor Legion. Let me contact Captain Hartmann at the base. See if there are any more reports of an energy weapon being utilized. We'll hurry."

As John Rourke finished speaking, Paul Rubenstein noticed something on the headsup display, long range radar data showing incoming vehicular traffic from both the north and the east. "We've got trouble, maybe."

The next instant, John Rourke was sitting beside him at the secondary console, Paul Rubenstein able to see him at the far right edge of his peripheral vision. "Looks like three vehicles from the north and another three from the east, Paul." He could hear John Rourke's fingers working over the computer console, summoning data. "Got it. The radar configurations match those of Soviet Armored Personnel Carriers, full track vehicles roughly thirty-five feet in length. Troop capacity is thirty-six, plus a two-man crew. All the data is tentative because they've just been introduced into the field."

"Great," Paul observed, not meaning the word the way he had meant it the last time he'd used it. "They're closing fast. How big are the treads, John?"

"A meter in width. They should be able to roll over almost anything. Michael?"

"Yeah?"

"Climb up into the gun turret. And keep something in mind, Michael."

"What, Dad?"

"If they've just been introduced into the field, these new APCS, they might have been introduced with the new armament. That'd give us six Particle Beam Weapons to face."

Paul Rubenstein could feel his armpits starting to get wet with sweat.

The headsup display showed the vehicles moving into some sort of attack formation.

"You got it, Paul?"

"Long as you want me to, John. Think we can outrun them? or at least outmaneuver them?"

"I have a feeling we'll find out very shortly, Paul."

Chapter Thirty-seven

Otto Hammerschmidt sat staring out the window set in the helicopter's sliding door to the portside of the fuselage. He said nothing, only stared. The window material was bullet-proof, of course, and slight distortion was evident in the image beyond it.

The dual (analog/digital) display Steinmetz on Darkwood's left wrist showed they'd been en route for a little bit more than an hour. These helicopter things were very fast, but Jason Darkwood had to admit they almost seemed to stand still by comparison to the J7-V vertical take-off jet fighter bombers of which the Germans seemed so justifiably proud. If he could get a submarine to move that fast— He smiled at the thought, but a glance again toward Otto Hammerschmidt, in fear for the life of his younger brother, forced the smile away.

Colonel Mann, tall, straight, his face open and friendly as it always seemed, the eyes clouded in thought or some problem that needed resolution, came aft and sat down beside him. "Captain Darkwood."

"Colonel."

"We will be reaching the rendezvous site in approximately seven minutes. From the information I have been able to obtain, it would appear that some sort of energy weapon was used by the Soviet personnel who attacked the Commandoes of the Long Range Mountain patrol. Sergeant Schlabrendorff, Lieutenant Hammerschmidt's senior non-commissioned officer, was worn and tired, not having slept for better than forty-eight hours, still insisting that he be allowed to return to the aid of young Hammerschmidt. He has been brought along, partially sedated. The two men are friends, you see. Rather like you and Captain Aldridge." Colonel Mann gestured toward Sam Aldridge, Aldridge asleep in the rear of the machine, snoring softly.

"Is there much chance young Hammerschmidt survived?"

"Very little, but he is a good soldier, so we shall not count him

144

among the dead yet." And he clapped Darkwood on the thigh. "I realize you are the veteran of many combats, but there could be intense fighting here. We must leave the machines and travel on foot for approximately two kilometers. If the KGB Elite Corps raiders who attacked the Long Range Mountain Patrol are still in the area, there could be considerable difficulty."

Jason Darkwood smiled. "I threw away the pills your friend Doctor Munchen gave me. My head aches like someone hit it with a rifle butt, but at least my head's my head again, if you know what I mean, Colonel."

Colonel Mann smiled, then started to rise. "Good man!"

Chapter Thirty-eight

Michael Rourke's eyes hurt from staring and he forced himself to blink.

On the horizon, becoming visible out of a swirl of snow from the north, he saw three of the six Soviet armored personnel carriers.

If his father were right (and that was usually a foregone conclusion), these might well be armed with the new Particle Beam weapons. What possible defense there could be against them was simple and obvious: run.

Running was exactly what Paul Rubenstein, still at the controls of the vehicle Michael's father had dubbed the "Atsack," was doing now. But in case that didn't work—Michael Rourke's hands moved over the dorsal gun's targeting computer controls, another heads-up display showing targeting data appearing in the bullet proof glass dome beneath which Michael sat. All six Soviet APCs were visible to the computer's sensing devices and, eyeballing the snow for visibility, Michael assumed that the second three would be visible to the naked eye in under sixty seconds.

He had only test-fired the Atsack's guns prior to leaving the German base where Vassily Prokopiev was hospitalized, but this test firing much like racking and firing a burst from the Lewis guns mounted on World War One vintage bi-wing aircraft. Yes, the gun system worked.

As to how well the gun system worked, he would shortly find out, Michael Rourke thought. He ran the computer for updated status on the guns, number of rounds, spacing of electronic tracer rounds.

And his palms sweated . . .

John Rourke sat beside Paul Rubenstein, watching the younger man's hands move over the Atsack's controls, Rourke's eyes glancing upward then, to the windshield and the heads-up sensor display there. All six Soviet APCs, perhaps fitted with the new Particle Beam weapons, were closing, boxing them in on the plateau.

Snow dispersed grudgingly before the Atsack, the all-terrain vehicle's three meter high wedge of titanium assaulting the drifts as if the snow plow and the snow were living things, locked in mortal combat spawned of hatred. But the wind blew at such velocity and the snow fell so unremittingly, that despite the titanium plow's tenacity each inch of ground taken from the wind-sculpted drifts was a major engagement.

The heads-up display showed more activity now, new Soviet T-91 tanks closing from the west, the Soviet armor so huge that were the Atsack and one of the tanks to be side-by-side, the Atsack, for all its immensity, would be dwarfed. There were at least a dozen blips on the heads-up display identifiable as T-91s, more blips farther away to the west, still not fully identifiable, the readouts on giving probability ratios, the percentages for correct identification rising: a weapon-system German intelligence overflights had only recently confirmed, its capabilities still not fully known, tactical missile launchers, designated AV-16s.

Suddenly John Rourke stood up, shouting to Paul Rubenstein, "Stop dead and kill all heat emitting systems and anything that makes noise or an electronic impulse. Do it now! It's our only chance."

Chapter Thirty-nine

He was not the victim of a crash. Of that, Natalia was certain from the first. The shrapnel wound in the young officer's left shoulder clearly showed evidence that the metal fragment—about three inches in length and better than an inch wide—had been stabbed in, like a knife would be. But the head wound was the most damning evidence. She had seen men beaten before, and he had been beaten, struck several times in the same area of the head, behind the left ear, with the proverbial blunt instrument. It was doubtful he had regained consciousness since. And, of course, there were the effects of the terrific cold to consider. He suffered from frostbite, hypothermia, shock.

He was in trouble. But they were in worse trouble, she knew.

"I've got him as bundled up as I can," Annie whispered, kneeling beside her in the meager shelter of the gutted German gunship.

"Then here's what we do," Natalia began, rearranging her head coverings against the cold. "I'll leave you here. They'll think I'm going back to the Retreat to get help to bring him in. So, they'll follow me and they'll leave some of their people to watch you. Unless they're stupid, they won't move against you, just in case they lost me, they'd want to be certain that when I bring back help I won't suspect something is wrong. I'll lead them in the general direction of the Retreat, then turn off and wait for them to catch up. You'll just have to have faith I haven't lost my touch," Natalia smiled.

Annie looked at her, pushing her hood back for a moment, tightening her scarf. "You're like Daddy. You were born with the touch," and she reached out and embraced Natalia.

Natalia smiled again. "If it works, I'll come back, circle around into the field out there and try to pinpoint their location."

"It's Rausch, isn't it, that man who wants to kill my mother?"

"Yes. I think so. From what your mother said, he must be very good, so we shouldn't underestimate him. He led your father on a merry chase and eluded him. Ordinary men don't slip through your father's fingers." Then she looked at the injured pilot. "Keep him as warm as you can. That's all we can do. If we can do this fast enough and well enough, maybe we'll get him back to the Retreat in time to save his life."

Natalia touched at the young man's face. He was a beautiful boy, and probably younger than she thought.

Then she looked out into the darkness as she pulled the scarf up over the lower portion of her face and tightened her hood. The men who had beaten this boy were hardly to be called men at all. And they were out there. She felt a queasiness in her stomach, wondering if she still did have it.

And knowing there was only one way to find out . . .

Jason Darkwood's knowledge of horses was limited to movie and television videos with such legendary stars as John Wayne, James Stewart, Clayton Moore, Jay Silverheels, Roy Rogers and Dale Evans. They rode proud animals, many with silver mounted saddles and names steeped in courage and romance—Silver, Scout, Trigger.

He'd asked if the horse he rode—neither a partly Arabian albino, nor brown and white paint nor a golden Palomino—had a name. He was told he could call the animal "Fritz."

No silver mounted saddle either, merely something that looked reminiscent of the McClellan saddles John Wayne and his men had ridden in all those cavalry versus the Indians movies filmed in that magically beautiful place called Monument Valley (Darkwood had kept company with a girl who was quite the student of film and television in the decades prior to the Night of the War and the trivia attendant to these productions had made interesting conversation at times). As they rode, Wolfgang Mann at Darkwood's right and Otto Hammerschmidt immediately behind them, Darkwood found himself humming Elmer Bernstein's famous theme from "The Magnificent Seven." But, in fact, there were forty of them, a thirty-six man Reinforced Long Range Mountain Commando Group, the colonel, Hammerschmidt, himself and a doctor skilled at treating for exposure, hypothermia and the like.

And they didn't ride to some distant village to save the people there from marauding bandits. Their goal was approximately ten minutes farther ahead, a high mountain plateau, a man who was probably dead and—somewhere out there, marauding to be sure—a KGB Elite Corps Commando Unit armed with a weapon that seemed too frightening to contemplate but, nonetheless, so frightening it could not be ignored.

"You are humming under your breath? A song you like?"

Darkwood looked at Wolfgang Mann, nodded, only just then aware that the theme had become audible. "Yes, but from very far away."

Natalia Anastasia Tiemerovna walked as deliberately as she could, never turning to look back, never taking her right hand from the climbing stick and shifting it to the pistol grip of her rifle (as much as every fibre of her being wanted to), her palms perspiring slightly inside her gloves.

She focused her mind away from the drudgery of the walk through the drifted high snow, away from the possibility that at any moment her unseen enemies would strike, preempt her own planned attack.

She thought about John Rourke, but not in the way she usually thought of him, as some unattainable romantic ideal, but as a comrade, someone she had learned a great deal from. His motto, of course, was "plan ahead." And she had done that as best she could. Her revolvers were visible to her watching enemies over her coat, as was the rifle, but the suppressor fitted Walther PPK/S .380 in the Null shoulder holster beneath her parka was not, and lashed with dressmaker's elastic to the inside of her left forearm so she could get at it quickly with her right hand (but could work it free with her left, if need be), was the Wee-Hawk blade Bali-Song lockknife.

She kept walking, the Retreat's main entrance, its access already drifted over with so much snow there was no sign that it was a human habitation, clearly in sight for split seconds at a time as the wind would shift for an instant and the blowing snow would dissipate.

John Rourke had planned ahead there, too, because the rough road leading up to the Retreat forked and she took the fork, walking past safety and security – the Retreat was all-but impenetrable – and moving deeper along the height of the mountain. There was a niche of rock there, perfect for her purposes.

If she could get that far . . .

John Rourke and Paul Rubenstein dropped into snow that was chest deep, the wind which blew it across the high plateau like a knife edge slicing through clothing and flesh to the bone, despite any preparations against it.

The Atsack was, for all intents and purposes, dead, although ready to instantly revivify, all systems off. And John Rourke was banking on a minor miracle. With the intensity of the snowfall, the constantly shifting drifts and the Atsack, once stopped sinking into the snow as snow, blown against it, walled around it, any radar profile might be obscured enough to be missed. The only system which was operable aboard the Atsack was the radar countermeasures package, computerized, calculating the frequency and strength of any incoming enemy radar emission and instantly duplicating it, in effect absorbing the radar signal rather than bouncing it back to its origin, then broadcasting an identical signal so there would not even be a radar shadow.

In theory, at least, the system worked like that. But if the combination of falling snow, drifting snow and counter-radar measures would work to so completely obscure the Atsack that the enemy combat vehicles would pass the Atsack by was another question, and indeed the stuff of which miracles were made.

Rourke's M-16 would be useless to him against the vehicles themselves, but if his plan worked he'd be close enough to their occupants for the assault rifle to be effective.

And have the secret to the Soviet Particle Beam technology . . .

Nicolai Antonovitch considered another sexual encounter with the beautiful Svetlana Alexsova, her blond hair fallen loose to her shoulders and her blue eyes just a little glassy as she sipped at her vodka.

They were alone in the hermetically sealed environment tent, but even while they were "off-duty," other members of the joint military and scientific team continued the attempt to make contact.

The helicopters which towed the enormous floating platform constructed for just this purpose floated idly on the surface of the ocean a minimum distance of fifty meters from the sides of the platform, ready to bring the platform to its next location or to evacuate the occupants of the platform if needed.

Despite the platform's size, it shifted as the surface of the sea shifted. Antonovitch had lost the feeling of nausea this caused early on, as had Svetlana Alexsova, but other members of the party had not. And so one hour changed into the next, one day into another.

And no answer from their possible comrades beneath the sea.

Svetlana, although she was using him, was very beautiful; and, although he doubted the depths of her passion, she was satisfying to him nonetheless.

As he started to get up, he heard the shouts from outside the tent. "We have made contact! A submarine. The red star!"

Nicolai Antonovitch finished standing, straightened his uniform. So much for passion.

Chapter Forty

Natalia Anastasia Tiemerovna kept her same steady pace as she crossed around the tight bend in the right fork of the road, some several hundred meters beyond the entrance to the Retreat.

But as she passed the bend, she veered left, swinging her Colt assault rifle forward and, along with the climbing stick, utilizing its capped muzzle as a probe within the drifts to find her footing as she pushed herself up from the trail.

If they were far enough behind her and the wind kept steady, her footprints would obliterate quickly.

She moved through the rocks now, as quickly as she could without more than ordinary risk of breaking a leg or twisting an ankle on the uneven surface below the snow. The niche. She angled toward it and dropped from sight of the path.

She rolled onto her back and looked up into the swirling snow, the snow within seconds covering over her goggles. Natalia smiled, already removing the M-16's muzzle cap, but keeping the dust cover closed against the snow . . .

Annie Rourke Rubenstein touched her fingers to the young man's throat beneath the blankets swathed around him. His pulse was very weak.

She made a decision, quickly opening her parka, then parting his blankets, sliding beneath them, holding the dying man's head to her chest, drawing his body close to hers, her own parka partially around him, then pulling up the blankets to cover them both. He had lost considerable blood and the cold, if nothing else, would kill him.

The young man groaned softly in pain and delirium and she drew him closer to her, her M-16 beside her, her eyes on the night . . .

Eight men in a classic Viet Nam era American Special Forces patrolling formation moved through the snow below here, their weapons at the ready, each guarding the other's back, the muzzles of their weapons rising and falling as they turned, never crossing the body planes of their fellows.

It was like a ballet, nearly that graceful; and, like ballet, it told a story. These men were very good and very experienced working with each other, a troupe, as it were, which knew each other's capabilities so well that they were anticipated and compensated for so automatically that they were almost like lovers well-used to each other's slightest desire, the cues which made them react so subtle that no observer would ever notice them.

Nazis, she presumed.

As a Russian, she had been raised to have no fondness for them, thought Stalin a madman in the privacy of her own mind, for ever having allied with them only to reap the wrath of their betrayal. And, history aside, these Nazis were no bitter memory spoken of by survivors of a previous generation.

They were flesh and blood and death.

Eight of them.

One of her.

She would have to lower those odds.

Chapter Forty-one

Otto's brother lived.

Perhaps miracles did happen, Jason Darkwood mused, watching as Wolfgang Mann, a cigarette freshly lit at the corner of his mouth, exhaled then said, "They are waiting for us, I think. Otherwise, they would have killed the young man."

"I agree."

"I do not think that we should disappoint them, do you?" And Mann's left eyebrow curled upward, something like a smile but without the lips.

"No. I think they're very deserving and it would be a crime to let them get away from here without us touching base, so to speak, showing them a little of your country's hospitality, which I, of course, look forward to myself."

"Do you like streudel?"

"Yes—I think I do."

Mann nodded, as if some great question were now resolved. "My wife made wonderful streudel. But it can be had in the commercial bakeries, not quite as good." And he looked away, all trace of a smile gone. "So much evil," he said. The snow fell in large, almost gentle flakes, the size of the silver Eisenhower dollars Darkwood had seen in the pre-war coinage display at the New Smithsonian at Mid-Wake. Everything was gray, and Darkwood supposed the scenery reflected the mood.

There was a crunching of snow and Darkwood turned around, Otto Hammerschmidt still beside his brother as a tent was erected around them, but Sam Aldridge (who had been with the Hammerschmidt brothers) approaching, coming to attention, saluting, Darkwood letting Colonel Mann return the salute.

"Colonel, Captain—young Hammerschmidt confirms, as best he can, that it was some sort of energy weapon. I have no idea what."

"Very good, Captain Aldridge," Colonel Mann nodded, slipping back from his apparent reverie. "Then we should start at once. To find it, and the men responsible for using it."

Sam Aldridge snapped, "Very good, sir. Should I order the men to mount?"

"Leave an adequate force to defend the temporary camp. Captain Hammerschmidt can be placed in command of the defense."

"Begging the Colonel's pardon, sir, but Captain Hammerschmidt requested specifically to accompany any punitive expedition."

Darkwood watched Colonel Mann's eyes. They seemed to beam. "Select a junior officer, then. Would you concur, Captain Darkwood?"

"I would, Colonel," Darkwood said emotionlessly.

Colonel Mann turned to face Sam Aldridge. "You have your orders then, Captain."

"Yes, sir."

"We leave in three minutes."

"Yes, sir!" And Aldridge saluted.

Mann returned it, Aldridge jogging off. "Listen up Marines and you German Commandoes, too! We're moving out! Lieutenant Klein!" Aldridge's voice gradually diminished as the distance increased, but Darkwood still was able to hear the interchange between Aldridge and the young officer he had picked for taking charge of the defense.

"Yes, Herr Captain!"

"Pick eleven men. You'll need two machine guns. Set up a defensive perimeter for one hundred yards surrounding the tent and the remaining horses. Hobble the horses. Then set up a fallback line with secondary defensive positions at twenty-five yards. Be ready for anything. Keep your mortars behind the twenty-five yard limit."

"Yes, Herr Captain!"

"He adapts to surface warfare well," Colonel Mann began. "Walk with me." And they started toward the horses, snow crunching under their boots. "I had read prejudiced accounts of American Marines, of course, as swaggering blowhards."

"They can be that," Darkwood laughed. "But you shouldn't try soliciting fair comments about the Marines from the Navy."

"I think the accounts I read were grievously in error."

"The Marines have always been tough and adaptable. They used

155

to be called 'Leathernecks'," Darkwood smiled. "The story goes that during the early post Revolutionary War days, they wore uniforms with leather collars. And that's probably true, but I personally feel they're leathernecks because they're damned near indestructible. At least if the Marines of Mid-Wake are anything like the Marines before the war." And then Darkwood reached out his hand and touched Colonel Mann's forearm. Mann looked at him, quizzically. "But, do me a favor, Colonel, never tell a Marine I ever said that. There's the honor of the Navy to be upheld."

Colonel Mann allowed a smile and brief laugh, then they continued moving again through the snow toward the horses, Sam Aldridge's voice bellowing orders behind them still . . .

The eight men had clearly lost track of her. She watched with curiosity as, still careful of their defensive posture, they had obviously conferred, arrived at a decision, then acted upon it.

They split into four two-man groups to search for her.

Natalia Anastasia Tiemerovna, Major, Committee for State Security of the Soviet, retired (five centuries ago, she smiled inwardly), watched such a two-man team now.

They had come up into the rocks after her, not knowing she was in the rocks, of course, but merely following their part of the search pattern. She promptly moved deeper into the rocks, leaving the security of her pre-selected niche, tightening the sling for her M-16 since she could not employ it without alerting the other six she had seen. And, doubtless, there were more of the Nazis lurking about near where she had left Annie with the injured helicopter pilot who had been used so mercilessly to bait the women from the Retreat.

Gunshots might trigger action there that could result in danger to Annie.

Natalia moved as rapidly as prudence allowed there in the high rocks, with narrow ledges, ice-slicked and snow-covered, the climbing stick her only means of testing a surface before trusting it for a footfall.

And she was outdistancing the searchers easily . . .

Sarah Rourke tromboned the action of the Remington 870 police shotgun. She had been exposed to a sufficient number of guns since the Night of the War that she knew — in spite of herself — volumes of the little details which comprised much of the knowledge of the firearms cognoscenti. The fore-end of the twelve gauge, for example, was from a Pachmayr kit, while the black synthetic pistol gripped buttstock was from Choate. The leather shell carrier (apparently modified to fit the slender wrist of the buttstock) was from Milt Sparks. She tried to remember its model name — "Cold Comfort," Sarah Rourke said aloud.

Marie Leuden looked up from the book she was reading. "What did you say, Sarah? Cold comfort?"

"I was thinking out loud. But, I guess a gun can be cold comfort, can't it? What are you reading?"

"Michael told me I should read the works of Ayn Rand." She held up one of the philosopher and novelist's most famous — and longest — works.

"Ten hundred and eighty-four pages in paperback," Sarah said suddenly.

"What?"

"I read that in paperback. I didn't agree with it. John asked me to read it. I suppose I'd agree with it more now. I think he grew up on that book, the Boy Scout manual and GUNS & AMMO magazine. And, come to think of it, there were a lot of times out there —" and she gestured toward the entrance of the Retreat "— after the Night of the War, before he found us, I wished I'd read those."

"The Boy Scout manual?"

"Sometimes more of GUNS & AMMO," Sarah smiled.

She began loading the 870's extended magazine with the German-made clones of Federal 00 Buck loads John kept for the shotgun. If something went wrong and someone who shouldn't got into the Retreat, it would be a shotgun job.

Experience had taught her that.

Experience had taught her a lot of things . . .

As the nearest of the AV-16's rolled past them, John Rourke, only his face partially out of the snow, spread his arms, slewing snow away from his body, half falling as he broke into what passed for a run in nearly chest deep snow — more a combination of lunging, falling, swimming and trying to stand—toward the nearly cruise-ship-sized Soviet tactical missile launcher.

He glanced left, and Paul Rubenstein was just beside him.

Soviet vehicles—the thirty-five-foot long armored personnel carriers, the impossibly huge T-91 tanks and more of the AV-16 missile launching platforms—surrounded them totally now. With the somewhat disorienting effect of the snowscape, the only thing that confirmed to John Rourke that the Atsack and Michael hadn't been found on Soviet sensing equipment or collided with by mere chance was that there was no enemy fire, and all of the Soviet battle vehicles moved onward across the plateau, as though nothing could stop them.

Up close, Rourke almost wondered if anything could.

They kept running, falling into the snow, picking themselves up, running again, the AV-16 almost past them. Its treads were his immediate goal, so broad and so deeply ridged and so rugged seeming that his plan just might work. And it was the only option they had.

Rourke drew the Crain LS-X knife.

A shaft of yellow from one of the AV-16's running lights bathed the snow around them, the light glinting eerily on the twelve inches of blade steel of the LS-X.

Paul drew the knife sheathed to his belt.

John Rourke had planned ahead.

The knife in Paul Rubenstein's hand was the replica of the five centuries ago Crain LS-I old Jon the swordmaker had given to Rourke's son, Michael.

The AV-16 mobile missile platform towered over them now, its enormous gray bulk like a mountain moving along on tank treads. Rourke swam his way out of a snowdrift so high it was nearly to his throat, a storm of snow more intense than anything natural lashing around them, churned into a whirlwind by the movement of the AV-16s, the tanks and the armored personnel carriers. Rourke threw himself toward the rearmost segment of the AV-16's left side forward track, shouting to Paul, "Now or never!" There was no way of telling if his friend could have heard him.

The LS-X in both gloved fists, John Rourke hammered the blade outward and forward into the massive tread, the blade steel biting deep, Rourke's entire body vibrating with it, his arms and shoulders nearly wrenched from his body as the tank-like tread continued rotating, huge clots of snow flung upward in its wake, half burying Rourke as he was lifted upward. Rourke's chest, the entire front of his body was slammed against the tread, his breath going in one giant, involuntary exhalation, the upward pressure on his arms collapsing his diaphragm, making it impossible to breathe. The effect was like drowning, snow literally burying him as he was dragged upward, lungs burning.

He was prone on the tread, moving forward with such rapidity that—In microseconds, he would be dragged downward, crushed beneath the tread as it bit into the snow.

His knife.

Rourke shook his head, trying to clear it, gulping air, his mouth filling with snow.

He pushed himself up, the tread rotating downward. He looked to his right. A massive fender-like appendage partially covered the tread and it was his only chance.

With all the strength he could force from his wearied muscles, John Rourke wrenched the LS-X free of the tread and jumped. His body slammed against the ice-slicked armor of the tread fender and skidded forward, Rourke inverting the LS-X in his hand and punching the skull crusher buttcap into the ice, wedging it against the armor plate, his elbows locked, arms rigid.

His body slammed to a halt.

"Paul," Rourke rasped.

Through the swirling snow, John Rourke could not see him.

Chapter Forty-two

Natalia slipped the heavier outer glove into a side pocket of her parka, only the skin tight silk glove liner remaining. Immediately, she began flexing her fingers to keep the circulation going.

Years ago—centuries ago—when she had adopted the Bali-Song as her personal edged weapon, she had realized that the ability to make it move as though it were some sort of living entity could be a vital asset in close combat. Because of her ballet training, she had been taught to play the piano, to develop her appreciation and sense of music. She had never felt herself very good at it, but when she'd first begun to use the Bali-Song, or "Butterfly Knife" as such a knife was sometimes called, she had returned to the piano in earnest, but wearing gloves, like the post-World War Two night club entertainer Hildegarde had. For the Bali-Song to move quickly, it had to be barely touched, almost fly through the fingers. And it was this deprivation of normal tactility she had sought to perfect with the piano.

Scales, that bane of all pianists, then the metronomically demanding works of Chopin. When her fingers would be so stiff and weary that they could barely move, wearing silk gloves again, she would work with the Bali-Song. At first, she kept the primary and false edge taped, still cutting herself at times. Eventually, the tape came off. Only after she could manipulate it fully while wearing the gloves did she remove them.

Her piano playing had improved markedly, although she would never play for anyone to hear, too self-conscious, too aware of her pathetic shortcomings on the instrument. But the knife. It moved almost as though it possessed a life of its own.

To touch bare metal with bare flesh in these temperatures would be insane.

The glove liners, as skin tight as the silk gloves with which she had practiced all those endless hours.

The knife was in her right hand.

She could not try a practice opening or closing, because the clicking sounds of steel to steel might be heard, despite the keening of the wind, because the two Nazis who were her quarry were mere yards from where she waited now to kill them. Suddenly, she heard the crunching of snow beneath heavy boots. She tucked back deeper into the wedge of rock where she hid, the Bali-Song in her right hand palm, her fingers still moving to keep them limber against the already numbing effect of the cold.

Vladmir . . .

A flood of bitter memories passed through her and she was colder because of them. He had even persecuted her in death. And John, with Annie's help, had saved her, ridden as a knight errant into the omnipresent nightmare which was drowning her, killed the one who was already dead, freed her from her tormenter.

But from herself.

Her right hand which held the knife shook, beyond trembling.

She could hear the two Nazis breathing, now, the telltale creaking of equipment. In an instant they would pass by her and she would have to act or die, and she might die even then.

She saw them, back to her. But there was no moral dilemma. At the instant she opened the knife, unless they were deaf, they'd turn toward her And she counted on that.

And the scarf over her mouth and nose, along with the snow goggles, would protect her from the blood.

The little finger of her right hand nudged the Bali-Song's lock back and up as the first three fingers pinched the lower handle half against the interior of her knuckles.

The knife came alive in her gloved hand, the upper handle half swinging upward and forward as her grip shifted, thumb moving beneath the following blade, the pressure of her thumb's interior venus mound against her palm all that held the knife now, her four fingers opening outward, intercepting the forward swinging upper handle half as the nearer of the two men turned toward her, eyes wide beneath the snow goggles, visible in the light of the second man's flashlight.

Her right arm moved upward in a gentle left arc and swung back toward her, gravity doing the work, the Bali-Song's primary edge severing the man's carotid artery which was exposed, of course, because of where she had positioned herself and the click-click-click sounds of the knife as it worked. She had planned that, all of it. The fabric of the parka hood and what clothing lay beneath that meant only a little extra effort.

He began to fall as she involuntarily squinted against the blood spray. But the clothing he wore diminished that and her goggles protected her at any event.

The second man was raising his assault rifle to fire. She wouldn't let him, of course, starting the swing upward as she virtually pirouetted there in the snowy rock cleft, her left palm outward like a shield, but really to distract his eyes for that vital instant. Her right hand rose at the end of her arm, as if it were weightless, the tip and the false edge catching at his toqued chin, across his scarved mouth, tearing the toque away completely now as she hooked his left nostril, drawing her right arm back, as though the knife were not a knife at all but a sword.

She hacked downward and outward as the man's scream started, his face turned to her right, his left, brought there by the cutting action of her knife, again the carotid on the right side of the neck exposed.

The Bali-Song cleaved downward, across the artery, slowing as its primary edge encountered the collar bone beneath the right breast of the parka.

She spun left, the Bali-Song in a swordsman's guard position, beside her own right breast, to compensate for his superior height.

But he was already falling into the snow, the flashlight tumbling from dying fingers.

Natalia stood there, holding the knife.

Not a sound was on the air except the rushing of the wind.

She breathed.

There were tiny speckles on her snow goggles.

She nearly knelt beside the nearer of the two dead Nazis, wiping her blade clean on his coat. As she stood, she broke the silence, the click-click-click of the knife.

Seconds was all it had taken.

They were dead. And she didn't know whether the thoughts which filled her were somehow evil — like the men she had killed were evil — but she felt alive again.

"I'm back," Natalia whispered to the night.

Chapter Forty-three

Paul Rubenstein was being dragged along the tread, wedged beneath the fender which guarded it, the back of his parka ripping, his M-16 caught in it, the Schmiesser, lashed to his chest, stoving him in, denying him breath.

He fought to move, wanted to shout, had no breath.

His hands wrenched at the borrowed knife, tearing it free as the tread dragged him forward. He had missed the first time, not thrusting the knife with enough force, pitched back by the tread, clear of the AV-16, half buried in a drift.

He'd caught his breath, made certain his numbing fingers still held Michael's knife, then charged toward the mighty machine once again.

This time, he stabbed the blade deep, wrenched from his feet so suddenly he almost lost his handhold. But he was too close to the bodywork of the machine.

There was a snap, the sling for his M-16 ripped away, feeling the gun as it impacted his lower back, slid along his legs.

He clung to the knife, reached out.

Something had him, powerful, viselike, his left arm dragged outward and upward. His legs and the rifle were inseparably wedged for an instant and he did scream. And he was going over, down with the tread into the deep snow in the path of the tactical missile launching platform's left rear tread, to be crushed beneath it.

He was hanging, swinging like a marionette on one uncertain string.

Paul Rubenstein looked up.

He stared into the face of John Rourke and he was jacked upward and onto the AV-16's ice-slicked superstructure.

Chapter Forty-four

Jason Darkwood sat with his back straight, feeling the motion of the horse—Fritz—beneath him, but aware of it only on the very edge of his consciousness.

On his right, rode Colonel Wolfgang Mann.

On his left, Otto Hammerschmidt was astride a strapping animal colored nearly like the Palomino Roy Rogers had always ridden.

Their German assault rifles were across the fronts of their saddles.

"We're idiots," Sam Aldridge announced.

"Yes," Mann agreed.

"For a good cause," Hammerschmidt nodded.

Sam Aldridge's voice, Aldridge on the far side of Hammerschmidt, added, "Four of us and God knows how many of them."

"I am glad this God you refer to knows, Captain Aldridge," Mann's voice returned. "But I wish that he would share his intelligence data with us."

They moved along a narrow defile, wide enough only for the four of them to ride, their horses abreast of each other, the creaking of saddles, the snorting of cold-flaring equine nostrils, the clopping of hooves, the subtle metallic murmurings of equipment, the crunching and slipping sounds of gravel dislodging beneath the snow, but otherwise no sound except when one of them spoke. "Maybe it wasn't such a good idea I had after all, Colonel," Sam Aldridge announced.

"Now's a really great time to think about that, Sam," Darkwood snapped.

Colonel Mann laughed. "It was brilliant. They know it is a trap of sorts, yet they cannot resist killing four officers and they feel tactically superior with their new weapon. If we survive, I shall recommend you to your General Gonzalez, your Marine Corps Commandant, for a medal. If we do not, well—"

Hammerschmidt, for the first time since news of his brother's possible death and the realization that the younger Hammerschmidt had miraculously survived, began to laugh.

Jason Darkwood eased the Lancer 2418 A2 in its holster, his eyes on the rocky overhangs flanking them on either side as they rode into the pass. And he thought about his western movies again, saying under his breath, "Gary Cooper, eat your heart out."

Chapter Forty-five

They solved the problem of Paul's coat as soon as they entered the AV-16 through an aft service hatchway and were spotted by an Elite Corpsman guard. John Rourke shot the guard once in the head with the suppressor fitted Smith and Wesson 6906 9mm, the slide lock on, the shot all but totally silent.

Rourke manually cycled the action, reapplying the slide lock as Paul shifted into the coat over his already empty DeSantis Slant Shoulder rig, pain visible in Paul's face as he moved his shoulders and back. "Not a bad fit, John."

"Lucky for him he didn't die for nothing," John Rourke observed.

They started forward, the smell of synth fuel residue strong on the air, blue wisps of smoke like fog around them. Despite the fact that synth fuel residue was not harmful to inhale, the experience was not any the less nausea-inducing. Rourke and Rubenstein kept moving, past the six by six by eight foot, nearly cube-shaped tool storage area and into one of the narrow tunnels at its far end. None of the tunnels was wider than the shoulder span of a healthy-sized man. Rourke glanced at his old friend. Despite the battering Paul's body had taken, he seemed all right, Rourke promising himself to carefully examine Paul for any sign of injury at the first opportunity after they got out of this. In Paul's right hand was the German MP-40 submachine gun, in his left the battered Browning High Power 9mm. The second Browning, not nearly so used, would still be under Paul's coat, probably chamber empty, just stuffed into his trouser belt.

The tunnel extended some ten feet, stopping at a door which was round, locked with the type of mechanism usually employed on the watertight doors of submarines and surface warfare vessels. There was a synth rubber gasket surrounding the flange.

"In the event of a gas attack?"

"Likely the reason," Rourke agreed, reaching out his left hand to try the wheel-shaped lock. It would move, and relatively easily, Rourke decided.

"Probably troop quarters. Dozen or so."

"Probably." Rourke stuffed the suppressor-fitted 9mm under his coat, weighing the possibilities.

"Like always?"

"Sure," Rourke nodded. "With this all metal structure, we could kill ourselves with the ricochets."

"That's what I was thinking. Pistols, right?"

"Safer in the long run. Accurate shooting is better shooting," Rourke smiled.

Paul Rubenstein laughed, safing his submachine gun, shifting the older High Power into his pocket for a moment, extracting the second one, working the slide, settling it in his left hand, hammer cocked, the safety off. Then his right hand gripped the older gun, his right thumb lowering the smallish Browning safety.

John Rourke's coat was already open; the two Scoremasters were wedged between his belt and his sweater-covered abdomen. He shifted them slightly. "Ready?"

"Yeah," Paul nodded.

Rourke smiled.

His hands moved to the wheel and he spun it fast, the locking bolts well-lubed, sliding out of their receptacles, Rourke's left hand wrenching the wheel to full open, his right hand shoving the door inward as he stepped over the flange, both hands flashing to his pistols as his eyes shifted around the chamber beyond the doorway.

Six men were lying in smallish bunks racked along the sides of the ten foot wide, cell-like structure which comprised living quarters for the defensive team personnel. Eight more men—he and Paul had miscalculated—were either sitting on the edges of the shelf-like cots or around a small bolted down table at the exact center of the room, along which on both sides were similarly constructed, bolted down benches—the dining room.

"Comrades," Rourke whispered by way of greeting, one of the gleaming stainless steel .45s in each gloveless fist.

Steam clouds were everywhere as virtually all fourteen men exhaled simultaneously.

Rourke stepped left as Paul entered and angled right.

For an instant, no one moved.

Then one of the Elite Corpsmen reached for a pistol on the table near his right hand and John Rourke shot him between the eyes. Everyone moved at once, Rourke farther left, out of the far right edge of his peripheral vision seeing Paul shift right, the Elite Corpsmen scrambling for assault rifles racked beside their cots, pistols in gunbelts on the cots or about their waists, Rourke's .45s firing almost rhythmically, the lighter, sharper cracking sounds of Paul's 9mms, the sounds of rifle bolts being racked, slides snapping forward, bullets pinging off the metal walls and bunk frames and the metal table and benches.

Both Scoremasters were empty, slides locked open.

Rourke didn't draw the twin Combat Masters from the double Alessi shoulder holster under his parka.

There was no need to.

"I've still got twelve rounds," Paul noted.

John Rourke nodded, then started to change magazines. In a moment, more enemy personnel might be coming and the guns might be needed again.

Chapter Forty-six

Natalia risked her radio. "Annie, can you hear me?"

"I'm reading you."

She asked for the code phrase they'd agreed upon, something they'd both felt no man would trip to. "Did you start?"

Annie's voice came back, slightly embarrassed sounding. "I feel a little bloated. Any time now."

Natalia smiled. Neither of them was expecting her menstrual period, and the code response meant that Annie was free to talk, not under an enemy weapon. Natalia spoke, "I have to keep my voice low. There were eight men. Now there aren't that many. There may be as many surrounding you. Be even more careful than you were. How is the young pilot?"

"He's alive; I don't know for how much longer."

"This won't be much longer. Out."

Natalia had set hers and Annie's radios to a frequency neither employed by the Germans nor the Russians. If all frequencies were being scanned, the transmission—out of necessity, en clair—might have been picked up. Otherwise, not likely. She would bank on the latter, but if the transmission were intercepted it made little difference.

There were enemy personnel yet to kill before she could even hope to go back for Annie. And time—and the young German pilot's life—was running out. Natalia pouched the radio and started moving again, the snow drifts deep, the wind high and obliterating her tracks as soon as she made them. She knew these mountains reasonably well. The enemy personnel could not. And none of them but one perhaps was as good as she was; it wasn't conceit, merely honesty. And that one—this Rausch person—would lay back until the last.

She kept moving . . .

Their horses moved single file, now, Wolfgang Mann at the head of the short column, Jason Darkwood behind him, then Otto Hammerschmidt followed by Sam Aldridge.

A second ago, Darkwood had thought he'd seen movement in the rocks to their right and slightly above them, but it could also have been a trick of his imagination.

Both Sam and Otto were in radio contact with the remaining twenty men of their force, ten behind them at the base of the long defile through which they had ridden now for some time and ten—by now they should have reached their destination—on the far end of the defile. When the KGB Elite Corps unit struck, Sam and Otto would signal for the two ten-man elements to close in. Then it would merely be a matter of holding on until help arrived. At most, as Colonel Mann had assessed it after Sam Aldridge proposed the plan, five minutes at a gallop. The J7-Vs were on call as well, and they would reach the site of any ambush in under three minutes.

Jason Darkwood tried to feel reassured. But five minutes, or even three minutes, could be a terribly long time, long enough certainly to die.

Colonel Mann's horse moved ahead, the V-shaped stream bed through which they rode rising sharply and flaring outward dramatically now into rippling waves of snow splotched granite. It was almost possible again for two men to ride abreast. And, if the Soviet force were going to attack, they would attack now.

Sam Aldridge started to speak. "If they're going to hit us—" The blast into the rock wedge on their left choked off all other sound. Darkwood averted his eyes, feeling rock chips pelting at him after a wash of heat blew across them like a wind. His horse, Fritz, reared and Darkwood nearly lost his rifle as he clung with both hands to the animal's mane and the pommel of the military saddle.

Fritz slipped as the second blast came, showering man and animal alike in suddenly melted snow turned to steam and a blinding spray of rock chips and dust, only Darkwood's snow goggles saving his eyes as he plummeted from the saddle. The assault rifle fell with him.

He hit the side of the rock wall and skidded downward, catching himself as conventional automatic weapons fire laced across the granite inches from him. Wedging his boot heels against a rock ledge, he stopped, drew his pistol, stabbing it upward toward the obvious source of the enemy fire, returning fire in short, two round semi-automatic bursts, what Doctor Rourke so picturesquely called "double taps." Sam Aldridge's Palomino bolted past Darkwood, Aldridge clinging to the saddle with both hands, his assault rifle slung across his back, his feet dragging over the icy granite defile. There was a burst of assault rifle fire and Darkwood glanced right. Otto Hammerschmidt, horse under perfect control with Hammerschmidt's left foot stomped on the reins, was half-crouched, firing upward into the rocks.

There was a flash of light and, instinctively, Darkwood dodged, not knowing where to, but reasoning that moving was his best option. The granite less than a yard from where he had been exploded, a shower of steam and dust and rock chips obscuring everything for an instant.

The energy weapon.

In the snow at the dead center of the defile lay Darkwood's assault rifle. He started for it, but another blast from the energy weapon vaporized it and the rock around it. Darkwood edged back, shouting over the din of conventional small arms fire, "Sam!"

"I'm all right! Got you covered, Jase! Run for it!"

Darkwood didn't think twice, turned, and started in a dead run for the sound of Aldridge's voice. Assault rifle and machine gun fire tore into the rock on both sides of him, the ricochets like a swarm of bloodthirsty insects surrounding him. His left sleeve ripped. He felt a crease of pain on the outside of his right thigh. He slipped, but from ice and the uneven surface beneath his feet, caught himself, ran.

Colonel Mann was firing from horseback, his animal rearing suddenly as conventional small arms fire cut a ragged swath along the rocky surface near its forelegs. Mann half fell, half leapt from the saddle, his assault rifle in his hands as he crashed to his knees, rolled, fired. Then he was up and running.

Darkwood could see Sam Aldridge crouched in the rocks where the defile widened, Aldridge's horse dead in the snow beside him, eyes staring blankly at nothing. Assault rifle fire tore into the animal's body, making it lurch as though somehow reanimated. Darkwood's own horse was racing toward him and Darkwood pulled himself up from the ground to which he'd slipped again a split second earlier, reached outward as he threw himself toward the animal and caught his left hand in the animal's reins.

Darkwood fell, dragging the horse down as well. Another blast from the energy weapon, the horse scrabbling to its feet, Darkwood grabbing at the saddle, throwing his right leg over as the horse stood, shook, then vaulted ahead along the defile.

Darkwood could see a trail leading upward, not much of a trail but with the energy weapon and the heavy conventional weapons fire they wouldn't last the three minutes, assuming that Sam or Otto Hammerschmidt had had the chance yet to use their radios and summon reinforcements. Darkwood realized he was still holding his pistol and he used the weapon now like a whip or stick and slapped it against Fritz's sweat-gleaming right flank.

He started the animal up the trail, toward the summit from which the energy weapon's fire seemed to originate. "Gyaagh!"

Jason Darkwood didn't know what "gyaagh" was supposed to mean, but a lot of cowboys had used the expression when exhorting their horses to greater speed in the western videos he'd watched as a boy. "Gyaagh!" And it seemed to be working.

Chapter Forty-seven

She waited the better part of ten minutes for the orders to be given for the six remaining men in the immediate vicinity of the Retreat to reassemble after fruitless attempts at contacting by radio the two men she had murdered.

And now it would have to be very quick and there would be no second chances. Because, if it didn't work, she would be fully exposed to six assault rifles and have only two six-shot revolvers for defense against them. That would not be enough. There wouldn't even be time to reach the suppressor-fitted Walther .380 beneath her coat.

Her own assault rifle and the rifles of the two dead men would not help either, because she would have to walk into the thing bare-handed. She had learned the technique from John. In these days, and in those days five centuries ago, no one expected to be braced in a stand-up gunfight as in the era of the American wild west, face to face, live or die.

She called out from the darkness, in German, intentionally stilted. "I have come to talk with you. I am without a rifle. My hands are empty."

The six men turned to face her as one.

She hadn't lied, after all, because her hands were empty and her rifle and the rifles of the two dead men were hidden back in the rocks. And so were her holsters, but not the belt she usually wore them on. The belt was cinched around her waist, over her sweater. The twin stainless L-Frame Smith .357s with the American Eagles engraved upon the right barrel flats were stuffed into the belt, in the front, just the way John did it with his Scoremasters.

And, if she could pull it off the way John did it, she'd live—maybe.

"I am coming out to speak with you. We have you surrounded and we wish to discuss terms for your surrender."

She kept her hands well away from her body plane, so they'd be visible. She was counting on audacity, too, the sheer audacity of proclaiming that the six heavily armed men were surrounded by a group of women.

One of the six took a short step forward, raising his assault rifle to hip level.

"Fire a single burst and before I fall, there will be more gunfire from the rocks surrounding you than you can imagine." It sounded rather lame, especially in intentionally clumsy German. But, in a way, that could be good. The more over-confident the six men felt, the easier they would be to deal with. "Which is your leader?"

The one who had stepped slightly forward spoke. "I command this patrol. Our leader has your friend surrounded. She will die at the slightest provocation."

That was a possibility, of course, however remote, that upon hearing gunfire and after attempting radio contact with these six, the men near Annie's position would simply do their best to kill her immediately. But, with these six alive, the situation had no hope at all.

She stopped when she was thirty feet from the six men. They were bunched up tightly, which was better for her. "Will you lay down your weapons and surrender?"

The man who had stepped slightly forward laughed and turned to look at the other five. Natalia Anastasia Tiemerovna reached for her pistols.

One of the five men behind the leader started to shout.

She double actioned through the Smith and Wesson in her right hand, the revolver bucking slightly in recoil as she shot the would-be shouter in the chest. He started to fall back as she fired the revolver that was in her left hand, hitting the self-proclaimed team leader somewhere near the thorax, the precise location of her shot hard to gauge in the poor light and heavy snow.

The revolver in her right hand—she snapped a shot into the man at her far right, his assault rifle starting to fire as she stepped away and left, then fired the revolver in her left hand, the first shot spinning him around, the second shot punching him into a chest-high snow drift.

Gunfire tore into the ground less than a meter from her right foot and she spun toward it as she stepped left, both revolvers at chest level, firing simultaneously, her ears ringing with the sound, the man who had fired at her sprawling back, dropping to his knees, his gun firing into the remaining two men. Natalia wheeled toward them, firing a double tap from the revolver in her right hand into the nearer of the two men, then a double tap from the second revolver into the last man, both men falling down dead. Ten shots, six dead. She breathed.

Chapter Forty-eight

Jason Darkwood leaned hard over the neck of his horse, the animal stumbling, righting itself, vaulting ahead along the upreaching trail toward the height overlooking the defile within which his comrades still fought for their lives.

The hood of Darkwood's parka blew back and he ripped the Navy-blue stocking cap from his head, the wind lashing across his face as he shouted the magic word again to Fritz, "Gyaagh!" He lashed at the animal with the reins, kicking his heels against its pulsating flanks, spurring Fritz upward along the ice-slicked granite. "Gyaagh!"

The energy weapon fired again. He couldn't see the flash, nor the resultant explosion, but could feel the concussion almost simultaneously with the blast which assailed his wind and cold numbing ears. "Gyaagh!"

The Lancer 2418 A2 was still bunched tight in his right fist. He made it that there were nine or ten rounds remaining in the pistol, reminding himself he should count his pistol shots as carefully as he counted the torpedoes aboard his submarine, the *Reagan*. "Gyaagh!"

The horse beneath him half jumped, half stumbled over a dislodged pile of granite slabs, down to its haunches, Darkwood half out of the saddle, his right foot on the rocky surface beneath them, wedging into the rock, pushing Fritz upward, "Come on, boy! Come on!"

Fritz lurched to a standing position, knees skinned and bleeding, Darkwood in the saddle again without remembering exactly how, digging in his heels, shouting the magic word again, "Gyaagh!"

Fritz jumped forward and into a dead run along the flatter rock-bed, a bend just ahead, Fritz's hind feet skidding on the ice, the animal nearly going down, regaining its balance, then into the bend and around it. "Gyaagh!"

As Darkwood and his mount rounded the bend, Darkwood's eyes narrowed against the icy slipstream around them despite the protective goggles, just out of reflex action; he saw the leading edge of the Soviet line.

Two of the Elite Corpsmen in their white snow smocks, rifles to their shoulders, wheeled toward him. In Darkwood's mind flashed visions of all the cowboys of his youth, their pistols flashing fire in their hands as they rode. He stabbed the Lancer 9mm past his animal's head and fired once, then again, then again and again, bringing one of the men down, sending the Elite Corpsman spinning back over the edge of the overlook, a scream rising, falling, dying.

The second Elite Corpsman fired. Fritz lurched sickeningly, falling, Darkwood half-falling, half-jumping from the saddle, hitting the rocks, skidding down into a snow bank, his right ear packed with the freezing white crystalline substance, his mouth filling with it, his goggles obscured by it. Another burst of assault rifle fire.

Darkwood wiped his left sleeve across his goggles as he spat snow, then stabbed his pistol toward the Elite Corpsman, firing it, again and again, emptying the weapon into the man's upper body.

The man fell down dead in a heap.

Darkwood clambered to his feet, slipping, righting himself, standing.

Fritz rose, shook, stood there, a long but not too deep looking bullet crease along the left side of the animal's chest.

Darkwood ejected the empty magazine from his pistol, putting one of the extension spares up the well in its place, letting the slide slam forward. Another blast from the energy weapon, perhaps as close as a hundred yards ahead of him. It was deafeningly loud, his eardrums vibrating with it. Darkwood scrambled over the rocks and out of the snowbank, his gloved left hand getting the snow out of his ear. He looked at the horse. "We'll probably both get it, fella. Wanna try?"

The horse, of course, didn't answer him. But somehow, Darkwood sensed Fritz was game if he was. Darkwood swung up into the saddle, caught up the reins. He hammered his heels against the animal's sides and Fritz started ahead, gathering momentum. More of the Elite Corpsmen were visible now, rising from their defensive positions. Darkwood fired his pistol at the nearest of them, killing the man or putting him down — Darkwood couldn't tell which — with a single shot.

Darkwood's animal seemed to be moving faster, the Elite Corpsmen swarming toward them all a blur. Darkwood fired into the blur of bodies, no time to count shots, rifle butts hammering at him, at the horse, bullets burrowing into his saddle, a slug tearing across Darkwood's right thigh and right hip. Darkwood slumped, did not fall. "Gyaagh!" The pistol was empty. Darkwood clubbed at the face of an Elite Corpsman as Fritz body-slammed the man.

"We get through this, you'll be the first damn horse to get a Congressional Medal of Honor!" Darkwood shouted. Then the magic word again — "Gyaagh!"

The energy weapon. It fired, Fritz rearing, Darkwood nearly losing his balance. Fewer than twenty-five yards now. Darkwood whipped the empty Lancer 9mm across his horse's sweat-glistening rump. "Gyaagh!" Fritz leaped, running, Darkwood low in the saddle as gunfire thundered around him. Darkwood was hit. He didn't know where. He was still alive. "Gyaagh!" A spray of froth from his horse's wide open mouth washed over him.

Darkwood saw the faces of the energy weapon gun crew. There was terror in their eyes. One of the Elite Corpsmen drew a pistol. Darkwood drew his knife, the duplicate of the Randall Smithsonian Bowie that his ancestor had carried in the pioneering days of Mid-Wake after the Night of the War — when all was all but lost.

Darkwood threw himself from the saddle as Fritz reared, Darkwood's mouth opening to scream, "Die, you son of a bitch!" as he threw himself over the Elite Corpsman with the pistol. Darkwood's right arm arced downward as their bodies met, crashing into the snow drifted granite battlement, the primary edge of Darkwood's blade impacting at the juncture of the left shoulder and neck, only stopping as the blade jammed against the collar bone.

Darkwood's left knee smashed upward, finding a target firm yet yielding, a rush of air from the Russian's mouth as he screamed pain and died.

To his feet, Darkwood lurched toward the energy weapon, his left hand closing over it. A cable, like ordinary coax in appearance only considerably greater in diameter, ran from the rear of the gun toward some piece of unidentifiable machinery. Darkwood's right hand still held the knife and he hacked downward with it, a shower of sparks, an electrical arc, the cable severing as Darkwood's fist released the knife and closed over the pistol grip of the energy weapon. It was about the size of a conventional machine gun, awkward for one man to lift up, raise over his head, heavy, out of balance.

A pistol shot close beside him, a burning sensation across his ribcage, then cold as he hurtled the energy weapon downward over the edge of the abyss toward the snow splotched granite below.

As men swarmed over him, he thought he heard the sound of German J7-Vs coming over the horizon. But the horizon was lost in darkness . . .

Annie Rourke Rubenstein sensed the movement around her, telling herself it was merely a combination of audio and visual cues so subtle that she wasn't aware of them on a conscious level. But whether that were the case or not—if she really sensed the movement of the men surrounding her with something beyond the five normal senses—they were coming.

She checked the wounded German flier's pulse. It was nearly too weak to detect. "Natalia," she whispered into her radio. "If you can hear me, they're coming. Hurry, if you can." If Natalia were very near, Annie realized, she might well have the radio turned off so an incoming transmission would not betray her position. The units could be worn with earpieces, but these were uncomfortable at best and, in the cold weather, even worse. And if Natalia had heard, Natalia might be unable to respond without betraying her position.

At any event, there was no answer.

Annie unwrapped herself and the soldier sufficiently from the blankets that she could wriggle out, covering him quickly, only his mouth and a portion of his nose exposed. And she was instantly colder. Her rifle beside her, she clambered over two seat backs and crawled on hands and knees toward the farthest edge of the helicopter wreckage within which she had sheltered herself and the German. The snow pants she wore felt uncomfortable and she shifted the waist of the pants a little. How men could wear trousers all their lives was beyond her understanding. She kept moving, along the edge of the wreckage, toward a spot just aft of the gutted cockpit which she had determined earlier would be the best defensive position in the event of attack. From this vantage point, she could monitor activity visually for slightly better than 270 degrees of the compass. The remaining ninety degrees—in bits and pieces were irreconcilable blind spots.

She removed her heavy outer glove, pressing it under her armpit to keep it closed and seal the body heat within, then ventured the partially stripped hand to her waist, opening the M-12 holster there and extracting the Detonics Scoremaster .45. The Beretta 92F she carried in the other holster had a higher firepower potential to be sure, but if she needed a pistol at all, it would be at very close range and the .45 ACP round—because of her father's influence over the years, she realized—was deadlier to her way of thinking.

Annie edged the slide slightly rearward to visually confirm a chambered round. The press check completed, she reholstered, this time cocked and locked. The pilot made a soft groaning sound, which, a few feet farther away, would have been indistinguishable from the wind which keened around them. There was a sudden movement from far to her right and she had the M-16 to her shoulder in the same instant, aware that her glove had fallen to the snow drift which covered a portion of the cockpit doorframe.

"Fraulein Rourke!"

The man had a white flag tied to the muzzle of an M-16. She smiled, wondering who it might have been who'd given it to him—maybe Commander Dodd of Eden Base. "It's Frau Rubenstein," she called back across the snow, dodging slightly right before she responded, tucking back left, in case there were some sort of directional microphone trained on her for the purposes of nailing her precise position to a sniper.

"I prefer your other name, Fraulein. I should not like to have to think of you as a Jew."

She dodged right again. "Rather my husband's a Jew than a damned Nazi like you!"

There was no response for an instant, only the howl of the wind; but the man with the white flag didn't move to cover. She retrieved her glove, pocketed it. At last, he spoke. "Very well, Frau Rubenstein. My name is Hugo Goerdler. I have been empowered by my superiors to offer you safety if you will surrender to me at once. Otherwise, you will be shot."

She didn't bother answering, tired already of shifting positions back and forth so a directional sound unit couldn't get a precise enough fix on her position. It was rumored that the Russians might, in fact, be working on a sound based sniper system, utilizing ultra-sensitive computer linked microphones that could pinpoint and then identify a target. The rifle was sighted through the computer and merely fired. Utilizing specially designed armor-piercing rounds, it would be possible to take out a target inside a wide array of structures by shooting through the walls. Because of the possible Soviet breakthrough, the Germans were working on such a device as well. She was happy that the inevitable gunfight wasn't a year from now.

"Frau Rubenstein! This is the last time I will ask you."

She couldn't pass it up. "Thank God for small favors."

The man who had identified himself as Hugo Goerdler walked back into cover. Annie tucked down as well as she could. The German aviator was protected by an aggregation of assorted pieces of heavy debris from the gunship, walled in with steel and charred seat cushions, as safe as she could make him when the shooting started.

The shooting started.

Chapter Forty-nine

Michael Rourke's eyes burned and his temples throbbed, but he could barely risk blinking his eyes, had to keep them focused on the electronics displays before him. The last of the Soviet AV-16 missile platforms with its entourage of monstrously large T-91 tanks and armored personnel carriers was rolling past him, according to the display and the feelings in his guts, one of the T-91s less than a yard from him. He could feel the ground vibrate beneath the Atsack. Was the snow which was drifted and blown all around the Atsack being vibrated off?

If it were, and someone aboard the passing vehicles noticed, he was dead. All that saved the Atsack from electronic recognition was the metallic mass of the armored armada surrounding him—too many signals to interpret, even assuming the Soviet electronics were backed by computers as sophisticated as the system aboard the Atsack. But visual recognition was another matter and, at the distance, potentially more dangerous because the Atsack, without the mounds of snow which Michael Rourke silently prayed still obscured it, would be impossible not to see.

The T-91 nearest him had rumbled past without slowing, without altering course—at least according to the heads-up display he still so unblinkingly watched.

As his own danger began to pass, his mind began to fill with thoughts of his father, John Rourke, and his brother-in-law and friend, Paul Rubenstein—aboard one of the gigantic AV-16 tactical missile launchers, if they weren't already dead . . .

Clanking noises and groans, of metal striking or pulling against metal surrounded them, the overall ambience of the tunnel-like rust brown colored tube through which they moved, its air clouded with noxious smelling gray-blue wisps of synth-fuel residue, like hell's boiler factory.

John Rourke's eyes narrowed as he neared the AV-16's control cabin, a Detonics Scoremaster .45 bunched tight in each fist, the guns along his thighs, hammers cocked, the respective thumbs of his right and left hands poised over the ambidextrous safeties, ready to drop them. Paul Rubenstein, a Browning High Power in each fist, nodded toward the blue-smoky blackness behind them. John Rourke glanced that way and nodded back. There were new sounds, sounds of booted feet moving along the tunnel.

They were trapped.

Rourke hissed an obscenity under his breath and he stuffed both pistols into his trouser band beneath the open parka, his hands moving along the ceiling of the tunnel, over the access panel there. What it provided access to he didn't know, only hoped. The panel was secured with Phillips head screws. He reached to the musette bag near his left hip, finding the tool he required, unfolding the Phillips blade, putting it to the first screw head as Paul moved deeper back into the swirling synth-fuel smoke trailers, ready to meet the men coming along the tunnel.

The first screw was out and Rourke pocketed it, his other hand already working on the second screw. Loose. Out. Pocketed. The third screw. He removed it. The fourth screw, his left hand supporting the panel cover as his right hand turned out the screw. The head was slightly burred. He closed his eyes, inhaled, exhaled slightly, applied more upward pressure to the screw head, at last turning it out.

The sounds of the men coming along the tunnel were louder now, closer.

Rourke removed the panel.

A maze of plasticized tubes and three gauges. The AV-16s ran synth-fuel to power a closed system steam system which turned the massive turbines needed to propel it and provide for the massive demands of electrical energy needed. If the AV-16 were mounted with one of the energy weapons, the system would have to be indeed quite powerful.

A lot of steam.

John Rourke signalled into the corridor, hoping that Paul was observing him. The three gauges. Rourke studied them intently. One was an emergency bypass. He turned the faucet handle-like knob beside the gauge and pressure immediately began to drop. He turned back to normal pressure. The next gauge and the handle below it monitored and controlled recirculating steam. The third processed incoming steam, directing it along an emergency routing system, as best Rourke could discern, and through the main system.

He heard Paul's voice whispering into his ear. "Six men. We start shooting, we'll alert the crew in the compartment there." Rourke looked at his friend as the younger man nodded toward the control room.

"I think I've got that under control. Be ready to get through that doorway into the control compartment as fast as you can."

John Rourke adjusted the emergency bypass control, his eyes moving to the main system route for the steam. If he split the pipe in just the right way—And it was only the modern equivalent of PVC.

"Be ready."

Already, Rourke heard voices from the six men.

"Have your flashlight ready, Paul. Better zip up and pull your hood as close around your face as possible. Don't leave any more exposed skin than necessary. Hands, too."

Rourke took his own advice, pulling on his gloves as well. The screwdriver tool went into the musette bag by his left hip. Then his right hand filled with the Life Support System X knife. He turned his face toward the tunnel space behind them. "Goggles," Rourke rasped, pulling up his own. Even with the precautions, if he miscalculated, he and Paul would be boiled by the live steam.

"Ready," Paul Rubenstein whispered.

Six men. The two in front began to sound the alarm as they raised their rifles. In Russian, Rourke shouted, "Run for your lives," And he stabbed the LS-X into the steam pipe, letting go of the knife instantly, just leaving it in the PVC-like material as a wedge to direct the spray of live steam.

"I've got the door!"

The lights blinked out in the next instant, a buzzer sounding, a panic light illuminating the tunnel red, with the steam filling the tunnel—Rourke held his breath—the place was more hellish than before.

His goggles were beginning to cover over with vapor, but he could just see the doorway, Paul beside it. Rourke's hands went to his mouth and he bit off his gloves as he drew one of the Scoremasters, stepping over the flange for the doorway, his other hand holding the old Kel-Lite with its German batteries. "Don't move!" Rourke shouted.

But the crewmen of the control cabin were already moving, stumbling in the darkness that was relieved only by two spot-like panic lights set in the low ceiling, guns in their hands. Rourke opened fire, killing the man nearest him with a shot in the forehead. Rourke's left wrist and forearm braced his right wrist, the flashlight in his left hand, the light and the muzzle of his pistol moving simultaneously.

He heard the sharp cracks of Paul's Browning High Power, seeing the hazy beam from Paul's flashlight at the far right edge of his peripheral vision as Rourke fired again, dropping another of the crewmen with a single shot to the thorax. A double tap into the chest and heart of a third man.

Rourke's flashlight beam swept over the room. "Your left!" Paul snapped. Rourke sidestepped right as he spun left, flashlight and .45 moving as one. An Elite Corpsman, an officer, a short barreled assault rifle in his hands. As Rourke fired, he heard Paul firing from behind him. The Soviet officer's body twitched back, then doubled forward as Rourke and Rubenstein each fired again, the Russian sprawling sideways over a control console.

"Paul! Get this thing under our control! I'm killing the steam and restoring power, then I'll lock us in!"

"Right!"

John Rourke rammed the nearly empty Scoremaster into his trousers, grabbing the second pistol, reaching the door. A man—recognizable as that only by the uniform and the gun—writhed on the tunnel floor near the doorway, nothing human-looking left to his red raw face and hands. Rourke shot him in the head.

Stepping over the body, Rourke drew up his goggles, the flashlight weaving crazily over the ceiling of the tunnel now, thrust into his belt but still on.

Gloves. Rourke pulled on the right one, then the left, goggles up. He'd burn himself, most likely. His left hand held the flashlight and he safed the Scoremaster, dropping the pistol into his parka pocket, eyeballing the target for his right hand while he could still see through his fogging over snow goggles.

Rourke reached into the steam from as far behind its jet as he could, pain seizing him as his double gloved hand penetrated the spray, his fingers closing over the emergency bypass control, twisting it, his teeth gritted against the pain, his goggles nearly fogged over now. Rourke retrieved his knife, hot feeling even through his gloves. His hand shifted, and he groped blindly for the tunnel wall, found it, moved along it, tearing down his goggles, a wash of cold air over his eyes and upper face.

He reached the door, the jet of steam slowing as he stumbled over the flange and pulled the door to. "John—"

The normal lighting had returned and the contrast to the hell-like exterior nearly blinded Rourke as he stared past Paul Rubenstein toward a Soviet non-com, an Elite Corpsman, in the man's hands an assault rifle. The man's left temple was bleeding, but he was otherwise unwounded.

Paul had both Brownings pointed at the Elite Corpsman, the Russian's rifle pointed at the AV-16's master control panel. The monitoring screens were between Paul and the Soviet non-com. On the monitoring screens, like massive windshields but functioning like the viewing ports with which Mid-Wake submarines were equipped—merely giant video screens—Rourke could see the terrain over which they sped. There was no sign of Michael in the Atsack, which was good. But the terrain was familiar. The AV-16 was speeding toward the edge of the plateau, hundreds of feet of sheer drop beyond and below it.

"John—"

The Russian, in English so colloquially intensive that the man had to be one of the men who had survived with Karamatsov, ordered, "Drop the damn guns, man, or I'll waste the control panel and we all go to hell! And you—the pig sticker. Ditch it now!"

"Pig sticker? You're obviously no connoisseur of steel, pal. This is a hand-made, marked prototype of a specially designed knife made for me five centuries ago by Jack Crain, one of the most famous knifemakers in the world. Pig sticker? Be serious."

"Drop it, asshole. You're Rourke, aren't you?"

"If you know I'm John Rourke, then you know what I'm going to do with this knife, don't you—asshole."

The Elite Corps non-com wheeled toward John Rourke, the control panel no longer his target, in the same instant Rourke's right hand moving forward in a long, fast arc, Paul shouting, "Down!"

As the LS-X flicked from Rourke's gloved fingertips—the pain to his flesh as his fingers flexed moving through him like a shiver—Paul's Browning High Power discharged simultaneously, the Elite Corpsman's body sprawling back, his rifle discharging into the control panel as Rourke hit the floor.

"Shit!" Paul snapped.

Rourke was up, moved toward the control panel, kicking the rifle from the dead man's hands as he retrieved his knife from the dead man's chest, two bullet holes in the Elite Corpsman's body, one in the chest inches from where the LS-X had struck and penetrated and one in the throat just under the chin.

"Hate throwing a good knife," Rourke remarked as he pushed the body to the floor, wiped the blade clean of blood on the man's uniform then leaned over the console. The AV-16's maneuvering controls were shot to pieces. They could be rewired—he looked at the view screens—but not in time. Less than four minutes and the AV-16 would be over the edge of the plateau. "Gimme a hand, Paul—fast."

"What do you want me to do?" It was less of a question than a request.

"See if you can bring up the locations of the rest of the vehicles in this squadron."

"Right."

Rourke crossed the compartment to what appeared to be the main computer console, began trying access names—"Missile targeting" brought up the program he wanted after better than one precious minute.

"John—got all the vehicles I can find located. Might have missed one. I don't think so. And we don't have Michael in the Atsack—that's certain."

"Hang on." Rourke's eyes scanned the program, his reading knowledge of Russian not nearly so good as his spoken command of the language. "Natalia," Rourke almost whispered. He missed her, for more than her Russian language skills.

He had it. "Try this sequence." And John Rourke began reciting a litany of number-letter codes, these in English, just the same way that Soviet missile bunkers before the Night of the War used English tracking symbols. "A-19; C-6; F-13; W-3; K-5; whatchya got?"

"Bingo! She's running."

Rourke's eyes left the green screen for the computer console, the whirring of the drives grinding in an almost reassuring harmony. He shifted his gaze to the heads-up on the view screens. Each vehicle Paul had located, displayed on the view screen by its sensor impression, was acquiring a target designation, one after the other. There was probably an override program which would allow the AV-16 in which they rode to target itself. But no time was left to find that. And the fall over the plateau would obliterate this machine at any event.

"Can you launch?"

Paul looked at him, saying, "They couldn't be—"

"They aren't nuclear. I got that out of the program. High Explosive Anti-Tank." Rourke smiled, then started for the door, his right hand stiffening, the skin cracking as he moved it within his glove. He pulled the glove away.

"Where you going?"

Rourke glanced at the view screens. About two minutes only remained until the AV-16 rolled over the edge of the plateau. As he doused his right hand with the German-devised antiseptic healing spray, he told his friend, "To the turret. I'll get out through there. Soon as you have those missiles launched, get the hell out of here. See you on the outside."

Rourke didn't wait for an answer, throwing open the door, a fresh magazine going up the well of the nearly emptied Scoremaster, the second .45, one round fired, still in his waistband. He jumped the body of the man he'd mercy killed, running along the tunnel now toward the center of the vehicle, ticking off seconds in his head.

Gunfire tore into the metal of the tunnel wall near Rourke's head and Rourke dodged the pinging ricochets, then threw himself down, the Scoremaster in his right fist stabbing toward the origin of the gunfire, an Elite Corpsman, the skin of his hands and face scalded. Rourke fired, then again and again, the Elite Corpsman going down, his assault rifle spraying across the tunnel ceiling, Rourke's hands and forearms moving up to protect his head, ricochets whining everywhere around him like swarms of bees.

As the singing of the bullets dissipated, Rourke was up and moving, running along the tunnel now, the partially shot out Scoremaster still in his left fist, his right hand nearly fumbling the tactical magazine change because of the pain there.

Rourke rounded a bend and neared the approximate center of the AV-16, an overhead hatchway there. Rourke started up the ladder, only three steps needed before he could comfortably attack the hatch locking mechanism. He wheeled it open, then pushed the hatch upward, licking his lips as he continued up the ladder. The only item of his equipment he considered expendable was the M-16—there were plenty of those. He loosened it on its sling and flung the weapon through the hatchway opening.

Pistol fire reverberated from above him as Rourke dove upward through the opening, banging his head on the hatch flange, but not seriously, stumbling back.

About fifty-two seconds remained before the AV-16 went over the precipice.

An Elite Corpsman, sitting in a reclining seat that was synchronized to turret movement of the energy weapon, a second man—a gunner's assistant of some kind—stood crouched beside a small control panel. Both men had pistols in their hands. Rourke's right hand moved to his waistband as the gun in his left hand fired, three 185-grain hollowpoints impacting the man beside the control panel, Rourke throwing his weight against the gun mounts, the gun shifting, the pistol shots from the man in the chair going wild, spiderwebbing two gauges on the control panel as Rourke's right hand—his flesh screamed at him—stabbed upward and his first finger flexed against the trigger twice, the first shot penetrating through the chair's left armrest, hurtling the man in the chair half out of it, the second shot entering through the left side of the gunner's neck.

Rourke safed both pistols as he spun toward the hatchway, kicking it shut as hands—one of the hands held a Soviet pistol—pushed through. There was a scream of agony, fingers severed, skittering across the floor of the turret like living things. Rourke reached to the floor, grabbing up the M-16, the buttstock penetrated several times by pistol shots. He wedged the rifle's barrel over the hatchway door.

Twenty-five seconds at the outside.

The energy weapon. Rourke reached for it, eyes moving downward, scanning for the mount system. A simple push through bolt secured with a large cotter pin. Rourke tore the cotter pin free, then pushed out the bolt. He wrenched the energy weapon free of the mount, a cable feeding downward from it through the mount.

Twenty seconds.

Rourke glanced overhead. The bubble of the gun turret was partially cocooned in titanium or something like it, partially only the interior covering, something like plexiglas.

If the material were enough like it—

Rourke pulled on his gloves.

The cable extending from the gun was well insulated. Rourke set the energy weapon on the seat, beside the dead man who was half-fallen to the floor. Rourke drew the Crain knife, realizing he might be destroying it.

His right foot braced the gun downward, the LS-X in both fists as he raised it over his head.

He focused his concentration through and beyond the tautly distended cable as he hacked downward. The knife caught for a split second, then cleaved through the cable in a shower of sparks, Rourke's hands opening, his body lurching back, slamming against the turret bulkhead.

The cable was severed. Rourke dragged himself to his feet. Ten seconds? He didn't know. Rourke's gloved hands reached for the sparking main section of the cable, catching it well down from the severed portion, holding it away from his face as he stretched it upward to the plexiglas-like substance, the still flowing power making contact with a steel bolt, the electricity arcing across the transparent material. It began to burn, flames licking outward so suddenly Rourke's right hand and arm were nearly consumed in them.

Rourke looked to the floor. His knife. He grabbed it up, the LS-X at cursory glance seeming none the worse for wear. Sheathing it, Rourke reached for the energy weapon. It was about the size of an ordinary pre-War M-60 machine gun.

There was a cracking sound, the sounds of metal straining against metal and he looked toward the hatchway as the M-16 bent and snapped away from the hatch opening. Rourke left hand stayed on the energy weapon, his right moving to his mouth. He bit his gloves away and drew the 629, double actioning it down the hatchway, the noise in the confined space of the turret deafeningly loud.

Rourke glanced to the transparent portion of the turret dome. It would have to be burned through enough.

As he stabbed the emptied .44 Magnum into its holster, he caught up the energy weapon in both arms like he would have carried a baby, clutching it against him as he stood on the gunner's seat. Flames licked toward him in the wind which lashed through the ever enlarging opening.

Rourke braced his right foot against the rim of the turret, fire searing at the flame retardant material of his snowpants. Holding the energy weapon with his right hand and arm, he reached his gloved left hand into the flames, screaming as he did it, catching hold of the titanium cocoon, hauling himself up, through, his parka on fire as he stumbled through the opening and down to the shell of the AV-16, wind tearing at him, snow blinding his ungoggled eyes.

He squinted against it as he rolled across the armored missile platform's hull. Tube hatches were open, steam and vapor rising from them, mass launch of the platform's missile complement imminent as he rolled his body in the snow there, trying to extinguish the flames.

He looked forward. The ground fell away, the AV-16 starting to lurch into the abyss.

His parka still aflame, the energy weapon clutched to his chest, John Rourke pushed himself up, dodging an open firing hatch, then another, near the tread fender now, the roaring starting, the groaning of straining metal that had begun an instant earlier as the AV-16 began to slip over the edge totally drowned out.

John Rourke jumped, flames all but consuming the sleeves of his parka, the legs of his snowpants, the missiles launching, the roaring of their engines numbing him as he plummeted through empty space.

John Rourke impacted something, suddenly smothering, his mouth filling.

Snow. Rourke burrowed into the drift, the battery firing of the missile complement continuing, the ground shuddering, then suddenly more explosions, the vibration of the ground beneath him became more intense. He tried to look up but he could not, was slammed downward by concussive force of explosion after explosion as the missiles reached the targets clustered around him, secondary explosions now as the weapons within the armored vehicles of the Soviet assault force themselves exploded. The ground seemed to break away from him. Snow showered down on him.

The flames were gone from Rourke's clothes.

The explosions kept coming . . .

Jason Darkwood opened his eyes. "You are a brave man, Darkwood," Wolfgang Mann smiled. Darkwood looked past Mann, seeing Sam Aldridge, left arm in a field sling, a silly grin on his face, beside Sam, Otto Hammerschmidt. There was a look of satisfaction in Hammerschmidt's blue eyes.

"Did we win?" Darkwood asked.

"You won, Captain. We only finished your work," Mann told him. Darkwood felt a little sick to his stomach and light-headed at the same time. He looked around him. He was inside a J7-V. He was lying down.

"You're gonna be fine, Jase," Sam Aldridge said, leaning over him, holding Darkwood's hands in his. "You saved all our lives and when we saw you pitchin' that damn energy weapon, we thought you were a goner. They did, anyway. Me, I knew you'd come out on top. You're banged up, maybe got some cracked ribs, got a few bullets that zigged when you zagged, but you're okay, Jase."

There was something important Darkwood wanted to ask. And he remembered. "Fritz—ahh—the horse."

"I'm sorry, Jase," Aldridge whispered, looking away as his voice cracked a little.

As Darkwood closed his eyes, his eyes began to fill with tears . . .

He couldn't hear Paul, but could see Paul's lips moving. There was a roaring in his ears. John Rourke told himself it would subside. The snow still fell, but there was a ring of fire surrounding them as Rourke lay there in the snow, Paul kneeling beside him. The flames, Rourke realized, were from the synth-fuel stores of the Soviet armored vehicles which the missiles had destroyed. In time, they would die out.

Rourke sat up, shakily but not with considerable difficulty.

He was wrapped in an emergency blanket. He assumed Paul could hear him. "Was I burned badly? I feel all right. I can't hear you yet, so nod."

Paul smiled, shook his head in the negative.

"I wasn't burned badly?"

Paul nodded this time.

He would have asked about Michael, but coming toward them from the furthest edge of the most distant arc of flames was the Atsack.

"Did we win?" Rourke smiled.

Paul Rubenstein smiled, nodded. John Rourke, his right hand still paining him, the wind blowing bitterly, snow mounded around them, reached under the tatters of his parka.

He found a cigar.

Rourke looked at his friend, the Zippo flaring in Rourke's cupped hands, his right hand still hurting.

Paul Rubenstein was laughing and it was like watching a silent movie, only the gestures, not the sound.

Rourke felt himself starting to smile as he thrust the tip of his cigar into the wind-dancing blue-yellow flame. The energy weapon lay in the snow beside him. With the plans Vassily Prokopiev had struggled to bring the Allies, now there was a chance against the new Soviet technology . . .

There were five men surrounding Annie, closing in on her position in an ever-tightening circle. As carefully as she could, Natalia scouted the surrounding terrain before assuming her position in the rocks above the road which fronted the field in which the gutted helicopter lay. There had been no sign of anyone beyond these five.

All of them were heavily armed, but that was to be expected.

Sporadic firing began against the helicopter where Annie stood watch over the wounded German aviator. Natalia brought the M-16 to her shoulder as answering fire came from Annie's position.

A good accurate rifle—a Dragunov, which she'd cut her rifle marksmanship teeth with; or, a Stey-Mannlicher SSG, like John used ("John," Natalia whispered almost aloud.)—would have been better suited to the task at hand.

As the five men advanced, Natalia settled the M-16 comfortably.

She touched her finger to the trigger in the next instant after Annie began again to return fire. Short bursts from the thirty-round magazine. One man down. Another man, but to Annie's fire. Another to her own. Poorly aimed shots tore into the rocks surrounding Natalia, but she kept her spot there, no time to move. She fired again. Another of the five men down, now only two remaining.

A heavy volume of fire from Annie's position. Natalia emptied her magazine, changed quickly to another, a steady stream of short, full-auto bursts, steam rising off the barrel of her rifle as snow melted from it.

Five men down.

The firing from Annie's position terminated, as did Natalia's. Natalia took her radio from her pocket. "Annie. Stay put for a while until we are sure. Do you read me?"

"Thank God you came. I'll stay put. He's still alive. So we can't sit it out for long."

"I think we have them all," Natalia said, breathing . . .

He watched the two women. On an improvised travois, slipping over the snow like a heavy laden sled (he had seen these in photographs from the days of glory in the true Germany), there was a body. It would be the traitorous and expendable pilot from Wolfgang Mann's command. If the pilot lived to enter the Retreat of Doctor Rourke, the man would die soon thereafter.

But the two women were going to the Retreat of Doctor Rourke. That was the important thing.

Beside him, Hugo Goerdler said, "Your plan is working, Freidrich. But it was wrong that thirteen of my men should die."

"You knew the plan. You approved the plan. Do not summon the rest of your force until we see them begin to enter."

"I sometimes think you forget, Freidrich, that you are under my command."

Freidrich Rausch laughed. "I sometimes think you forget, Hugo, that I do your dirty work so well"

Freidrich Rausch returned his gaze to the two women as they struggled along the road toward a peculiarly shaped mountain in the distance.